BEST KEPT SECRET

Skye Warren

CHAPTER ONE

Jane Mendoza

THE WORDS HANG in the air.
Hello, Jane.

Fear freezes every limb. It stops my heart. It turns my breath into ice.

Emily Rochester isn't supposed to be here, alive and breathing. She's supposed to be buried in Maine. Paige's mother, the woman Beau Rochester once loved, is dead.

It's not a dead woman who studies me with a fierce resolve.

I remember her from faded Polaroids inside an old journal. She has the same delicate features, the same blonde hair. She's beautiful by any standard, but there's something frayed about her appearance now. Her cheekbones are too defined, as if she's lost weight. In the photos her expression was solemn. Even melancholy. Now she looks like a warrior in the heat of battle.

And somehow, somehow I'm the enemy to be conquered.

"Hello, Emily," I hear myself say over the pounding of my pulse. "How did you get here?"

"The same way you did. By plane. Or do you mean how did I get into your apartment? I told your roommate I was with the apartment complex. Poor girl didn't wonder why I didn't have my own key. She was too busy on her way to some restaurant for work."

My laugh comes out hysterical. "I meant how did you get to be…alive."

"Ah," she says, her expression neutral. "That."

"Your daughter mourned you. How could you abandon her?"

Anger flashes through her blue eyes. "Abandon her? You have no idea what I've done to keep her safe. You don't know a damn thing about me."

I bought the desk chair she's sitting in from Goodwill a year ago. It was wobbly even when I brought it home, but it only cost ten dollars. She stands, as elegant and regal as if she were rising from a throne.

My pulse speeds up.

She isn't holding a weapon that I can see, but

her mere presence is a threat. The fact that she lied to get into my apartment. The fact that she followed me to Houston.

"Then tell me," I say, my throat dry. "Tell me what you're doing here."

She looks out the window, which overlooks the parking lot. She would have seen Noah's truck drop me off. A shiver runs through me.

I felt like this the night I saw that woman walking on the beach by the inn. That was Emily, wasn't it? It was her on the beach in a nightgown. I saw her hair in the moonlight. She could have seen me. With my hand pushing back the curtain, looking out.

I'm sweating in my long-sleeved shirt and yoga pants. These clothes are made for the cool spring of Maine. My heart is still there, along with Beau and Paige. It must be some other organ that pounds in my chest now, a million miles a minute.

One shoulder lifts in an elegant shrug. "It's a long story."

"I have time."

A ghost of a smile. "I see why Beau likes you."

"He doesn't *like* me. I was an employee to him. Someone to take care of his niece."

Her eyes shutter. "How is Paige?"

I shake my head, bewildered. "Why don't you ask her yourself?"

"If only it were that simple."

A wave of chills runs down my spine. She knows too much about me—where I live and what I've been doing. And I know so little about her. Her cryptic responses don't tell me anything.

My bedroom is too small. There's no space to breathe, let alone think.

"I'm going to go. I think it would be best if I left." Never mind that this is my apartment. I'll start walking and call Noah as soon as I'm out the door. I'll run if I have to. I'll abandon these clothes that aren't right for Houston and the suitcase that's not right for this neighborhood and flee.

The corner of her lips turns up. "How rude. You haven't even offered me refreshments."

I take a step back to the hall. It's not far to the front door. "I'm leaving."

She opens her purse with a graceful flick of her fingers and takes out a gun. Emily slides her thumb over the side, and something clicks. When she points the gun at me, her hands don't shake. This woman is comfortable holding a gun.

The blood in my veins freezes. Every part of me goes still. Emily Rochester is a dead woman.

Except she's alive…which means she's been hiding for a long time. They held a funeral for her. "There's no—" My tongue feels numb with fear. "There's no need to threaten me."

"I'm not," Emily says. "I'm showing you why you're not going to leave." Those ice-blue eyes meet mine over the black blur of her gun, and they blaze with desperation. She looks as desperate as I feel. Why did I ever get on that plane? Why did I ever come here? I should have just disappeared. "You're my only hope to get my life back."

"What are you talking about? I'm no one." It's fear that makes me honest. One twitch of her finger, and I'll be dead. Murdered in my Houston apartment. No degree in social work. No new life away from Beau and Paige. Death, and then nothing.

"Beau never was good with sharing his emotions."

The casual way she talks about him makes my heart beat faster. For a different reason. Jealousy. How laughable. I have no right to be jealous over him. "I don't know what you think's going on between me and him, but he sent me away. He fired me."

"To keep you safe. I could be upset, I suppose, that he's concerned for your safety, when he couldn't be bothered about mine. But I never really told him everything, did I?"

"Listen, I don't know what happened between you two but—"

"It doesn't matter. Him and me? We're nothing. I'm not here as your rival."

"Then why did you bring a gun?"

"I've been carrying this around for months. Ever since..." She trails off, and for the first time, a flash of stark emotion crosses her beautiful face.

Her grief reaches across the small room. It wraps around my throat and squeezes. "What could have happened? What could have made you leave Paige if you didn't actually drown?"

She closes her eyes. In that moment I could run. I could probably make it down the hallway before she shoots me—and maybe she wouldn't even shoot. Maybe it's just an empty threat. Part of me thinks so. But I don't run. I want to find out what happened.

I want to find out why Paige Rochester believes she's an orphan.

Because I remember the searing pain of that. The cold knowledge that I'm alone in the world.

"I didn't fall off that boat. I wasn't pushed, either."

"Let me guess. You jumped."

"I don't trust Joe Causey." She frowns a little. "My own brother. Though it's hard to think of him that way anymore. He's like a stranger to me. A stranger who murdered Rhys."

My mind processes this news like I'm watching an episode of Law & Order. "Joe killed him," I echo, because what else do I say?

"That night on the boat. They had a falling out. Joe and Rhys—they used to do business together, and they got into a fight. It was a bad fight. The kind of fight that partnerships don't come back from. Joe confronted him at the dock. I saw them arguing." Her voice shakes. "Joe shot him in the head, and I jumped in the water."

"God."

The desperation in her eyes makes her look hunted. "I couldn't come forward and be with Paige. If I turned up alive, Joe would kill me and take her. I was the only witness to the murder. I can't go to the police about it. Ever. Any police. Joe already has them in his pocket."

I wish I could deny the point, but the truth is that cops protect their own. In the foster care system you hear about it. They'll protect Joe before they take Emily's word for anything. "You've been watching us," I say, feeling slightly breathless. "Why didn't you tell Beau?"

"Tell Beau?" She lets out a high, bitter laugh. "I don't trust Beau, either. He rejected me. He put me in that situation in the first place. I never would have gone back to Rhys if Beau hadn't turned me away. We could have done anything. We could have run away, and I never would have been in that damn boat."

Maybe she's right. I don't know. All I know is that arguing this point with her won't get me anywhere. "There's time to figure this out."

"There's not," she snaps. "There's no time. My daughter thinks I'm dead. Joe Causey could find me at any time. And if he finds me, it's over." Emily takes a half-step toward me, the gun aimed at my chest. I let go of the suitcase and put both hands up. If I calm her down, I can get out of this alive. That's what matters now.

"This isn't the solution." I pretend with everything I have that she's Paige, overwhelmed by her emotions and not fully in control of herself. The first thing to do when a child is melting down is to bring them back to calm. There's no reasoning with someone who's on the edge like this. "Emily. Put the gun down and we can talk."

"If I put the gun down, you'll run away, and you can't do that."

"We're not going to fix this by shooting people."

She doesn't lower the gun. Not at all. Tears gather in the corners of her eyes. "Am I shooting you? I'm not shooting you. You're going to listen to me. There's no one else to do it."

"To do what?" Spots of pink turn to red high on her cheeks. Emily looks more like Paige with every moment that passes. It makes my heart ache for the little girl I left in Maine. "Listen to you? I hear you. I hear everything you're saying. I just think there's a better solution. I think you should talk to Beau." She hasn't interrupted me yet, so I keep going. "He's—he's a good guy."

Even if he did send me back to Houston.

"No. No." Emily's eyes narrow. "He's not a good guy. He had a rivalry with Rhys, but that doesn't mean they aren't the same. Beau is just like him, in the end. He won't help. He'll just tell Joe that I'm alive, and then I'll be hunted down and killed."

"That's not true. He wouldn't do that."

"What do you know about Beau Rochester?" Emily's lip curls. "Or did you think that sleeping with you made him a good guy? You're the nanny. He hired you to take care of my daughter, and then he went after you. Is that what good men do?"

Her words sting, because they're true. What Beau and I had together probably wasn't right. Rich men shouldn't sleep with their nannies. Nannies shouldn't fall for their wealthy, brooding bosses. But it happened anyway. And now my foolish heart wants more of it. I don't know which thing hurts more. Knowing Beau and I were destined for disaster, or knowing that I fell for it anyway.

"He cares for Paige." At her daughter's name, Emily's face softens. "Just like you care for Paige. That's your common ground. He won't do anything to hurt her. He won't turn you in to Joe Causey. He hates Joe Causey."

The gun moves down an inch.

"You know Joe went after him after the house fire. He tried to blame me and Beau for it. He made everybody sit for interviews, even Paige. You know Beau hated that. He doesn't trust Joe, and he won't screw you over like that. You need to talk to him."

"He won't help," she says flatly, but the gun lowers another inch. If she shoots me now, I might not get hit, or it might only graze me in the hip. "You're going to help."

"What kind of power do you think I have?" I

gesture at the room around us. The falling-apart furniture. The threadbare carpet. "This is all I have."

"You're close to him," Emily says. "You're the nanny he broke his rules for. You're the one he went after. The one he wants."

"He doesn't want me." I stifle my own bitter laugh. "If he wanted me, I wouldn't be here."

"Please. He wants you more than anything. That's why he sent you away. Beau Rochester just likes to suffer. It's his way of being the hero. Trust me, I know." Old hurt darkens her eyes. "You think he didn't want me? He was trying to be noble, and look where it's gotten us. Rhys is dead, and I might as well be unless I can solve this problem."

"I don't know what you want me to do." I feel like screaming, but I keep my voice soft and even. Like I would for Paige. "This is a conversation that—"

My phone rings in my pocket.

The bright, cheery ringtone is wrong for this moment, almost comically ridiculous, and my cheeks heat with embarrassment. I must not have turned the phone on silent. I always kept my old phone on silent. I don't have my old phone anymore, or my old clothes, or my old life. I might not get a chance at my new one, either.

I take it out of my pocket.

There's Beau's name, printed across the screen in big, bold letters. My throat aches at the sight of it. I have no idea what he's calling for. What he could possibly want from me. He already got everything he wanted, and then he sent me away like it was nothing. It probably was nothing. It had to be nothing, if he could put me on a plane to Houston without a second thought. Put all that money in my bank account and sever the ties between us.

Except this one.

I bring my eyes back up to Emily's. "It's Beau," I tell her.

She lifts the gun, aiming it squarely at my head. "Answer."

CHAPTER TWO

Beau Rochester

JANE'S NOT ANSWERING her goddamn phone. I've never had a reaction like this to unanswered calls in all my life. Cold sweat. Hot anger. If I could run to her right now, I'd do it, but she's on the other side of the country. I sent her there to keep her safe.

The threat to her life had never been more obvious. A dead rat on the porch. A slip of paper with her name on it. *Jane.* And I'd bought in to the idea that the only thing to do was send her away. Mateo spoke the words. *Anything else happens to her, and you'll be on the hook for it. You won't be able to live with yourself.*

I'm not sure how I'm supposed to live with myself now.

Christ. She hadn't been gone three hours when Joe Causey showed up with proof that

Emily's still alive.

Now all these words are a storm in my mind. *Maybe this is your chance. If she's still alive, you could be with the woman you wanted all along.*

I didn't want Emily. I wanted the idea of Emily. I wanted everything Emily represented. Money. Success. Stability. I got those things without her, and they still weren't enough. Nothing was enough until I met Jane Mendoza.

Jane, who isn't answering her phone. She needs to know that Emily is alive. She needs to be on the lookout. Emily's not going to go to Houston—she's been in Eben Cape all this time, and there's no way she skips town to go that far. But I won't keep another secret from Jane. The Rochester secrets have already been too deadly.

Paige sits silently on the sofa at the inn, staring at the TV with no discernible expression. I know I should talk to her. I should sit down next to her and ask simple questions about whatever the hell she's watching until she opens up to me. How do people live like this, constantly torn between expressing their love for one person or another?

I love Jane, and it's dangerous. It's always been dangerous. When Rhys was alive, loving anyone meant bringing them close to the volatile toxicity that defined our relationship. Now that he's dead, the secrets that surrounded him—and me—are impossible to escape. I love her anyway.

Beyond that, I have a duty to keep her safe. It's why I made her get into that car in the first place. I fired her from the job and paid her full salary to keep her away from the inevitability of me wrecking her life. That's what always happens.

My jaw clenches. My teeth are going to be ground to stubs by the time she answers. *Answer, Jane. Christ. Pick up the phone before I lose my mind.*

I dial again.

Voicemail. Kitten pads through the kitchen, winds through my feet, and leaves again.

Hearing her voice drives a dull knife through my heart. She even sounds optimistic in her recorded message. I dial her number again.

"Hi!" Jane says. "You've reached Jane Mendoza. Sorry I missed you. Leave your name and number, and I'll call you back as soon as I can."

It kills me to hear it. Jane's voice in this recording is warm and hopeful and it makes me think of her, everything about her—her dark hair, her dark eyes, the way she flushed whenever I touched her. The sound of her moans. Goddamn, I want her. And I want her here, where she recorded this message. It's the new phone I bought her after the fire. She spoke these words outside with the rush of the ocean in the background. When she says number, Paige says, *Jane, look in the distance.*

I hang up.

Dial again.

It rings.

I go for the front bay window and search the street, my heart pounding. One ring. Two. She's not out there. No car pulling up. I didn't think there would be, but it's a way to hide my face from Paige. If this call goes to voicemail now—

"Hello?"

Jane. It's her. Her tone isn't bright and warm the way it is in her voicemail greeting. It's cautious. Tentative. Brave, like it was the first night she came to Coach House. She was soaking wet from the rain, terrified and pretending not to be. Jane arrived after dark. It must have looked like a horror movie with the rain coming down around her. With the cliffs and the house looming above her.

And me.

I loomed over her, too. Pissed off and frustrated. Acting like an asshole. One look at her was all I needed to know that her dark eyes would be my undoing. Bracing one hand on the windowsill keeps me from collapsing under my relief.

"Jane." Come back. I want to write that on her body. COME BACK TO ME. "Are you okay?"

There's a pause on the other end of the line as she weighs the question. "Yeah? Why do you ask?"

"Where—" It doesn't matter where she is. I don't need the address; I just need her safe. "Is your front door locked? Does your bedroom have a lock on it?"

"Of course it's locked." Now she sounds like she's trying to soothe me. It's how she'd speak to Paige when her frustration ramped up and threatened to get the better of her. "My bedroom has a lock on it."

"Make sure it locks."

There's a noise in the background like she's jiggling the knob. "It does. Why do you want to know about this?"

Damn it. I can hear in her voice that she's tired. She's been crying. Probably about leaving Paige. I know better than to think the connection between them wasn't real. I know better than to think I'm not hurting her by placing this call. No amount of rationalization will change that truth. I've had to hurt her to keep her safe. I'm having to do it again now.

"Joe came over. He thinks Emily is alive."

"What? That's—that's crazy."

"Yeah. I thought so too." I've felt like I was going out of my mind since I got the call that they were dead. "But he has her on camera. It's grainy security footage, but it's her."

"Hmm." Again with the soothing. Again with the calm. "It could be anyone, really. I don't know how reliable that kind of footage is." This was a mistake. From beginning to end, it was a mistake. I should have fired her months ago. That was the time to admit I wanted her with me all the time, and not in a way that could fit into a boss-nanny relationship. Now she's somewhere I can't see and can't even begin to imagine. Some shitty Houston neighborhood that's so far out of my reach, anything could happen. "Why are you calling me about this, Beau? You don't care. Like, you sent me away."

I pace away from the window, my hand in my hair, a death grip on the phone. Frustration burns across my belly. "I wanted to keep you safe. I sent you away to keep you safe."

A slightly hysterical laugh bursts out of her. "Listen, either I'm in your life or I'm not. You have to choose. And you know what? You already did."

She's right. She's right. If she's safe there, I should in fact let her go. I should end this call, and I should let her go.

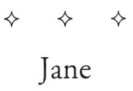

✧ ✧ ✧

Jane

EMILY'S IN MY ear, close enough that I can smell the faint floral scent of her. Close enough that I can feel her anxiety vibrating in the air. She can hear Beau's low voice through the speaker.

I've had some experience keeping my cool in impossible situations.

This has managed to blow through my composure. I'm shaking. I never imagined that I would be having a conversation with my boss, with my *lover*, with the man who rejected me, while I was being held at gunpoint.

How's Paige? Emily mouths. Her whole body is tense.

I raise my eyebrows back in the universal expression for *this is insane.*

Her eyebrows rise. *It wasn't a request.*

My eyes flutter closed. "How's Paige?"

"She'll survive." The truth is in Beau's stressed-out voice. It's gravelly and pained.

My heart squeezes. It took so long to gain

their trust. Beau doesn't like to admit it, but he's been through things, too. Paige isn't the only one whose life got turned upside down when her parents died. Now it's happening again.

It must feel like her nightmare is starting over again.

It certainly feels like mine is starting over. Losing my father. Being plunged into the foster homes, which were dingy and sometimes dangerous. It feels eerily close to what I've experienced in the last twenty-four hours. Beau and Paige became my family. Now I've lost them. And I'm facing a woman with a gun.

"You're safe?" Beau asks, a thread of concern in his voice. I don't understand it. If all he wants from me is confirmation that I've locked the doors, then he's already too late. Emily is in the apartment. There's no getting her out until she wants to go, and I'm pretty sure she's not just going to leave me here to live my life in peace.

The thought of Paige suffering hurts, too. She doesn't deserve another minute of pain in her life. So maybe it's a good thing that I walked away. It drew this madwoman away from her. If I don't survive this encounter, at least I'll have done that much. "I'll be fine," I say.

"Good. Stay that way."

There's finality in his voice, and I realize this may be the last time I ever speak to him. What will he feel when he finds out I was shot? Guilt, probably. I wish I could spare him that. Emily steps closer, eyes narrowed. She points the gun at the floor, but what would it take for her to lift it up and end this? Nothing. If this is the last chance I ever have to speak to him... "I don't blame you, you know. None of this is your fault."

A harsh laugh. "I fired you, Jane. Are you trying to make me feel better about it?"

"Maybe." That's love, I think. Wanting to spare him even as I ache. What a strange moment to realize I'm in love with him. When I can't possibly tell him.

"Don't."

I swallow hard.

"If anything happens—"

"I'll call," I say, my voice tight. I don't want to hear his worry for me. Don't want to imagine what's going to happen at the end of the call.

The phone disconnects.

We stand there at an impasse. Is she going to shoot me? Maybe. In a way she feels too rational, too sound for that. Then again even rational people can be dangerous when they're backed into a corner. I put my hands up to show that I'm not fighting, but I do take a step into the room. And then sit down in the chair that she vacated.

"Cards on the table, Emily."

She lifts a perfect, blonde eyebrow.

"Lay out your cards. You want my help? Then I need information."

A shadow of defeat falls over her. "You won't believe me."

"Try me."

"No one believes me."

There's the ring of truth in her voice. She's been silenced for so long. No wonder she's armed. It occurs to me that I might face this kind of thing as a social worker. That would have been after years of schooling and training. But I haven't gone to college. I have to face this on my own, with only my own experience, my own empathy to guide me. "Here's the deal. I want to hear your story. I want to believe you, but I'm not going to take you to Paige while you're holding a gun. If you want to shoot me? Then shoot me. You can't take a dead body on a plane."

CHAPTER THREE

Jane Mendoza

SHE DOESN'T SHOOT me.

Instead, Emily puts aside the gun and looks me in the eye. "My brother killed my husband. I had to hide to save my life. I couldn't spend any of the money. Couldn't bring any attention to myself. But when you left, I had no other choice. You're the only one who can talk to Beau and help me get Paige back. You're my only chance."

She stops. Swallows.

"I need your help. I want to see my daughter again, and I can't do that if I don't survive this."

She means it. Her desperation doesn't make her story less true. In fact, it makes me believe her. A person like Emily Rochester would have to be in dire straits to do this. She'd have no other options left. And something inside me knows this is real. "You don't want to hurt Beau?"

"I just want my daughter."

I glance at her purse. "No more guns."

"No," she promises. "Please come with me. I need to get back to her."

"I need to know that you won't do anything to hurt Paige. Even if that means…"

"I know," Emily says. "I know it won't be easy. Beau has custody." There are ramifications to all that. Legal ones. "I won't do anything to hurt her. I would never do that."

I should turn her down and stay at this apartment, but it already feels like the wrong place to be. It's a too-small outfit that's not in season. And this is about Paige. This is about believing Emily, who has never been believed in all this time.

That's how I end up back at the airport less than three hours after my plane touched down on the tarmac. It's equally as disorienting as landing here in the first place in all my clothes from Maine, because this is a part of the airport I didn't know existed.

Emily brought me here in a car I'm not sure is hers, but she doesn't drive it to the departures lane or any of the parking lots. Instead, she takes a narrow road that loops us around to the back of the terminal. A plane waits on the tarmac, far from everything else.

"That's a private plane," I say, because it is.

I've only ever seen them in the movies. It sits away from the airport with its own staircase rolled up to the side. It's significantly smaller than the plane that brought me here from Maine and significantly shinier. This plane has been polished to a high shine.

"Yes," Emily says, her voice grim. She's been resolute ever since we left my apartment. She drives her car onto the tarmac and throws it in park.

"Are you going to turn it off?"

"Are you honestly worried about the car? Let's go, Jane."

I get out of the car, and two men in uniforms move past us on the way to the trunk. Emily waits while they carry my suitcase onto the plane. It occurs to me that this is how she carried a gun through airport security, using a private plane. It might also be how she's concealing her identity. I suppose money opens a lot of doors that aren't available to regular people.

Emily takes the stairs first. On the way up she drops her keys into the hand of one of those men. He jogs back and gets into the driver's seat.

My old apartment felt wrong. A private plane doesn't feel right, either.

I'm beginning to think I won't belong anywhere now that I've known Beau Rochester. A voice in the back of my mind whispers that the only place I belong is by his side. But how can I belong with him if he doesn't want me there? I can't. That's the answer.

Emily lowers herself into a cream-colored leather sofa and tips her head back.

"Where should I sit?"

"Wherever you want," she says, her eyes still closed, her face tipped to the ceiling.

I choose the seat across from her. And anyway, the flight crew is shutting the door on the side of the plane. "How do you afford all this?"

Emily shifts to lean her head on her hand. Unlike me, she doesn't seem out of place here. Emily Rochester is the kind of woman who belongs on private planes. Beautiful. Sophisticated. Even on the run for her life, she looks classy.

Meanwhile I'm wearing jeans and an old hoodie.

The difference between us is so striking that it makes me dizzy. Not a great sign when you're about to fly. I focus on the open window behind her until I don't feel like I'm tipping forward off the edge of the earth. "With the money Rhys hid."

"Hid from who?"

She sighs, resting her hand over her eyes for a second before she drops it back down to her lap. Emily's tired. "Scary people. His accounting firm did well, but not well enough to make that kind of money. I should have known. Why didn't I know?"

The question seems rhetorical, so I don't bother answering.

"Rhys wanted more. He always wanted more."

In the neighborhood Noah and I lived in, people killed each other for money.

It always came down to that. Who had borrowed and who needed to pay. We imagined that if we had enough money, we wouldn't have to worry anymore. The more I exist in Beau's world, though, the more I realize that's not the case.

Even people with money die trying to get more.

"Who did he cross?"

A grim smile. "My brother."

The man who showed up in my hospital room after the fire. The one who accused me of using Beau for money. Only later did I learn he was

Paige's uncle. "He...killed your husband?"

She swallows hard. "Shot him in the head and pushed him in the water. I would never have believed it if I hadn't seen it happen. Unfortunately, no one else would believe me either. He's a respected policeman. I'm just a woman they've seen on domestic disturbance calls."

I know from firsthand experience how people don't believe the victims. How, too often, they blame the victims. As if it makes them feel safer, pretending we're liars. Pretending we deserve whatever happened to us. "I'm sorry."

"That's why I need you," she says softly. "They put women in two categories, you know. The Madonna and the whore. You're the virginal nanny who Beau fell in love with. I'm the crazy wife in the attic."

"You're not crazy."

"No one else will believe me. Even Beau turned me away."

"He'll believe you this time," I promise, even though I can't know that for sure.

"He will," she says. "Because he'll believe *you*."

I shake my head, but I don't argue with her. Beau doesn't love me. He sent me away. And there's a very real chance that he always loved

Emily. That he'll jump at the chance to be with her once he knows she's alive. His brother's out of the picture now.

They can be together.

I lean back in the plush leather chair as the plane begins to move. The pilot's voice comes over the intercom. "It's an honor to have you aboard today. Weather's clear, and you're flying today on a Gulfstream G-100. Wheels up as soon as the airstair is disengaged, and we'll be landing in Maine in a little under five hours."

Emily's eyes are closed again. Her head rests on the cushion. To an outsider, it might seem like she's asleep. I know different. I can feel her focus radiate from her body. I doubt she's slept much since she jumped off that boat.

My chair is easily a hundred times more comfortable than the one I sat in on the way to Houston. It's probably more plush than first-class seats. Meanwhile I sat in coach. "What's your plan when we get there? Are we both going to show up at the inn?"

"You'll go there." Her voice breaks. "I don't want to let Paige see me until I'm sure I can come home. I don't want to get her hopes up."

I let out a sigh. "As an orphan, I can assure you that her hopes are already up. They never really go away. I always dream of having parents."

She pushes herself fully upright, straightening her back. "Then help me fix this."

"How?" I ask, stress bleeding into my voice.

"Beau cares about you more than he wants to. I saw the way he looked at you."

I shiver. I can't help it. "How long were you watching us?"

"I've been watching Coach House all along." A flash of lighting in her blue-sky eyes. "I had to make sure Paige was okay. That she was taken care of. So I've been watching. It wasn't really a surprise that Beau delegated that to a nanny. The surprising part was that he was still involved. That the three of you became a family."

I can hear the hollowness in her voice. "Hey. Beau was there for Paige when she needed him, but he will never replace you. You're her mother. No one can replace you."

A smile flickers across her face. A blink and it's gone. "Maybe," she murmurs.

I try to keep my tone soft and casual. "Do you still care about him?"

"No." The answer comes so quickly I know she's lying. Or she's not telling the full truth. "And he doesn't care about me. This isn't about that."

I don't say anything, but my doubt must be in my face.

"I'd been watching you, mostly to make sure Paige was okay. Then when I saw how Beau cared about you, I realized I could use you. That if I approached you, if I could just explain what happened, you could help me convince Beau. Then you left."

"I was fired."

"You got too close to him. He cared about you too much, and he's running scared. That's even better. I need all the ammunition I can get."

I raise an eyebrow. "Even if he does care about me, I don't see how that's ammunition. I'm not a weapon. And Beau isn't your enemy."

"He's not my friend. I know he's told you about me. I know you've heard the infamous story of the white knight Beau Rochester turning me away because it was the honorable thing to do. He'll turn me away again." Her face turns pale. "That's why it's such a bad idea, Jane. It's a terrible idea to go to him alone. He would tell Joe. He'd tell the police department."

The plane accelerates, engines getting louder. We speed down the runway and lift off. Emily folds her hands in her lap. When the landing gear loses contact with the ground, she takes a deep breath. Her hands tremble. "I hate this."

"Flying?"

"Everything being so out of control." Her eyes come back to mine, huge and blue and rattled. More so the higher we get into the air. It's like when she was in my apartment. She was wild. Unpredictable. That will be even worse if it happens thirty thousand feet above the ground. "All I want is my life back. I want my baby back."

"We'll get her back." It isn't a promise I can make, but I say it anyway.

Concern splashes itself along the inside of my chest. Emily seemed composed when I saw her in my apartment, but she's not. She's barely holding it together. The shaking hands. The gun. All of it points to a woman so desperate she'll do anything.

Emily's life has reduced her from the elegant woman I saw in those photos to a wild-eyed, shaken person. It had to have been horrific to see her husband murdered in front of her. Horrific and complicated. Maybe there was a moment when she felt relief, knowing that Rhys was dead. But his death had also left her vulnerable. Her brother had proven himself to be capable of killing in cold blood over money. She survived with heartbreakingly limited options.

And for what?

For Paige.

"You might not be enough," she says, almost to herself. "You might not be enough to convince him. We'd have to come up with another plan, then."

"Even if we can convince Beau, how can he help?"

Her chin trembles. She looks so much like Paige in this moment. She looks lost and angry and hopeless, and I understand that. I felt that way in the foster homes with Noah. The difference between us is that I could cry on Noah's shoulder and let him tell me silly jokes and live to face another day. Emily doesn't have anyone. She's been hiding, trying to stay alive, and now her secret has been blown wide open. It must feel like she's running out of time. "My brother has the whole police department wrapped around his finger. They'll never believe me, and they'll cover for him when he kills me. Beau can stop them. He has power, connections, money."

"You have money," I point out, gesturing toward the private plane.

"A bunch of dirty money I don't even want. And can't even use. What am I going to do? Book a room at the Four Seasons? Joe would find me for sure. I've been living on canned beans and rice in a friend's cabin. The only reason I booked the plane was because you left."

"Emily, are you sure—is there any chance there hasn't been a misunderstanding between you and Joe? Something he kept back from you?"

"He shot Rhys in the head. He would have done the same to me if I hadn't jumped off the boat. I know, Jane. I saw it in his eyes."

She's so sure of it. But then Emily's also sure that Beau cares about me. If she's wrong about Beau, she could also be wrong about her brother. I don't know if I want her to be wrong on both counts or right. What I do know is that the plane is cresting the clouds. We're going back to Maine, and to Beau, either way.

Emily Rochester is a broken woman.

As broken as her daughter was when I first came to Coach House.

As broken as I was when I was in the foster care system. Maybe all of us are broken in our own ways. Maybe we're all running from the demons in our past.

I get up from my seat and move to hers. And then I reach for her hand.

Emily stares down at it like she's never seen a human hand before, then looks up into my eyes. "What are you doing?"

I push my hand toward her another inch.

After a long, breathless moment, she puts her hand in mine. It's cold, though we've recently been in the Houston heat. She's freezing to death.

"You're going to get through this."

Her chin dimples. "Am I?"

"Yes. I know it feels like you've been doing this alone, like no one will believe you, but that isn't true. Not anymore. I'm here with you. And I want what's best, not only for you, but for Paige. She deserves to have her mother back. She deserves a mother who isn't terrified for her life."

Emily takes a pinched breath. "I had to stay away. Do you understand? I had to stay away, and it's been killing me." One tear falls, then another and another until she's weeping. "I'm sorry. All this—I'm sorry, Jane. I should have come to you without a gun like a normal person."

"This isn't a normal circumstance." Emily's eyes are the brightest blue, just like Paige's, and they shine with her tears. "You must be so tired."

She laughs through a sob. "I can hardly sleep. I should have gone farther than Eben Cape, but I couldn't bear to be so far from Paige. I've been waiting for Joe to find me and finish what he started. Now he knows I'm here. I don't have much time."

"Listen." I squeeze her hand. "I want to help you."

"You don't have to. I wasn't going to shoot you no matter what you said."

"I know. But I mean it. I'll talk to Beau. I'll tell him what you told me. I'll help you. You don't have to do this by yourself anymore."

Emily pats my hand and wipes at her eyes. "I don't know what I was thinking."

"You were thinking of Paige."

"Yeah." She looks me in the eye. "I was."

"So." I get up and go back to my seat, giving her room to breathe. "Imagine we have Beau on our side. What's next? How will he use his power, connections, and money to help fix this?"

It's clear she's thought about this for a long time. "I need to get proof of what Joe's done. Not only killing Rhys, but all the smuggling and bribes. I won't be able to live any kind of life unless he's brought to justice. It's my only hope."

"And then afterward?"

Her expression clears, and Emily looks me in the eye with fresh determination. "I'm going to get my daughter back. I'm going to be Paige's mother again."

CHAPTER FOUR

Beau Rochester

THE SMELL OF burnt butter simmers in the air. A stack of blackened sandwiches sits on a plate beside the stove. An angry red mark across my forearm shows where I'd run into the smoking pot. That's it. Grilled cheese sandwiches defeated me. I can admit that. Kitten's the only one who's eaten so far tonight. She's still over by her food bowl, surveying the scene.

"I'm not that hungry," Paige says.

She's lying to make me feel better, which is a strange form of improvement. It's been seventy-two hours since Jane Mendoza was driven away from the inn. I expected Paige and me to devolve into the furious battles we'd had in the beginning. Before Jane taught us how to behave in a civilized manner.

I use the spatula to lift my latest attempt.

Black. "I don't know why they keep burning."

She offers a grim smile. "It's fine."

We've been on our best behavior, both of us pained and stoic in our grief. We want Jane back, for different reasons. Paige wants a caregiver who knows how to cook grilled cheese.

And I want the woman in my bed.

Oh hell, why lie about it? We want her back for the same damn reason. Because we love her. She became an intrinsic part of this family. There's no single word that encompasses her role here. Mother. Wife. She was neither of those things, technically, but she was so much more than a nanny.

"Why did Jane leave?"

Because I sent her away. I can't tell Paige the reason for that without scaring her. I'm starting another grilled cheese. I'm going to try adding more cheese this time.

"It was better for her to be home."

"She was home with us."

Paige folds her arms over her chest. Somehow, I'll keep this grilled cheese from burning. I don't know how I'm supposed to convince Paige that Jane belongs anywhere but here. She'll never believe it. Maybe she's right.

"Are you going to leave like Jane did?"

My chest feels like it's cracking. I put down the spatula and face her. There's true worry in her eyes. "No, sweetheart. I'm not going to leave. Not ever."

This is the thing that haunts me the rest of my goddamn life. First Paige's father died, and her mother left her. And then I sent Jane away. Why wouldn't she expect the same from me? "Everyone else did. Even Jane, and she said she wouldn't."

"Well, I mean it. I'm not going anywhere."

"Prove it."

How could I prove something that happens in the future? "I am going to prove it, Paige. By getting this grilled cheese right. You need to eat something. It's dinnertime. Marjorie left us some crab salad in the fridge if you want to try that in the meantime."

"I'm allergic to shellfish."

"Since when?"

"Since Jane noticed I got rashes on my back after eating it."

Christ. "I'll tell Marjorie not to make that anymore."

Paige rests her head on her small fist. "I need to finish my homework anyway."

Her hair is a wild tangle of blonde curls. There's a smudge of something on her cheek. She was never this much of a mess at the dinner table when Jane was here.

It's not a surprise that we need her. I knew it even when I sent her away. Maybe that was why I was so determined she should go. For her own safety, yes. And for my peace of mind.

I can't need anyone. It will only be harder to lose them.

With a damp paper towel, I gently wipe the dirt from Paige's cheek. I run a hand over her hair, taming it by the smallest percentage. She accepts my ministrations with a solemn expression. The silence throbs with the unspoken plea: *please bring Jane back.*

We've had this discussion, of course. Paige cried and begged, and I said no. She knows the answer will be the same if she asks again, so she doesn't even try.

This child is entirely too accustomed to loss.

"History?" I ask, my voice gruff.

"Math," she says, and I hold back my wince.

Last night's homework with three-digit division nearly destroyed us. It's not enough to come up with the correct answer. You need to show your work using the confusing new methodology the teacher taught. I didn't think it was possible but they changed math. It's different than it was decades earlier when I learned the same thing.

The printed worksheet is filled with fractions. Five eighths plus three tenths. *Thirty-seven over forty*, my mind supplies, but I know it's not enough to have the answer. She has to show her work, and there's probably some new way of doing that, too.

"Let's look at the YouTube channel," I say, resigned. Her math teacher has a video for each lesson showing precisely how she wants the work completed.

From the kitchen I can hear someone arrive. The bell above the front door rings. Marjorie left a few hours ago on some mysterious errand. And Mateo is taking an evening run along the beach. They're the only people who have the code to the front door.

The video loads the intro animation, featuring numbers as various jungle animals. We've only gotten to the monkeys and the elephants before something lifts the hair at the back of my neck. Awareness ripples through my body. I look up. It's not Marjorie with her hands full of shopping bags. Not Mateo covered in sand and salt spray.

Jane breezes into the kitchen, as casual as if she walked out an hour ago.

Paige's mouth drops open. This is what they

mean when they say *eyes like saucers.*

"You're here." I say it like the end of the explanation I was going to give Paige. It doesn't make any sense.

"I'm here."

"Hi, Paige."

Paige closes her mouth, still staring.

"I need to talk to you." The words come out of my mouth, and my mind supplies several possible endings. Forever. Always. For the rest of my life. "Out in the hall. We'll be right back, Paige."

I gesture Jane out of the kitchen and around the corner, push her back against the wall.

"You shouldn't have come back here." All I want in the world is for Jane to be where she is right now. Within reach. "I told you to leave."

"I had to come back."

"You didn't have to."

Relief rolls over me, crushing the air out of my lungs. Something essential moves back into place. I wasn't whole without her. Every goddamn thing was wrong.

"Yes, I did, Beau."

"You were safer where you were."

"No," Jane insists. "I wasn't. But I am now."

She looks into my eyes, and I see it. Something changed. There's a confidence about her. Jane is sure. I want to believe her. I want to hold myself back. For all of a second before I kiss her.

CHAPTER FIVE

Jane Mendoza

Beau kisses me with the desperation of an ocean surge. I thought I might sink down to the ground if he kissed me again. I thought I might not be able to stand it, but instead it makes me feel like the cliff near Coach House. Solid and strong no matter what rain lashes on the rock.

"Jane?"

I break away from him and step back into the kitchen doorway with a wave. My heart is going a hundred miles an hour, but a few deep breaths settle it. He didn't escort me to the door. He didn't throw me out. Emily is still out there, waiting for me to do this, and Paige is perched at the kitchen island, waiting to see if I'm going to walk out again.

Beau breezes by me with a light touch on my lower back that propels me back into the kitchen.

He goes back to the stove, and I turn back to Paige. From the way she's looking at me now, I belong here. It doesn't seem to matter that my contract with Beau is over. Technically, he's fulfilled his part of it. All of his money is sitting in my bank account.

It feels too dirty to think about that money now. Everything at the inn's kitchen is still the same. Beau moves between the stove and the sink. He bows his head over the dishes like they're the most important project of his life. I know they're not. He's done many things that are more important. His dark eyes flash up at mine and he lifts his chin. He's handsome. Windswept. Devastating. Even while he runs water and adds soap. I don't let myself think about how similar this is to a life we could share. There's only this moment, right now.

Paige tracks me, her arms tight to her chest. She's wary, if not outright suspicious. I don't blame her.

"How was your day?" I ask. "Did you go to the beach?"

She turns her face a little. Not quite looking away. Definitely refusing to answer.

"You flew here?" Beau asks. He's concentrating on the sink, but he steals a glance at me.

"Yes." On a private plane. With Emily. "Was it not a good beach day?"

"We went," Beau answers.

Paige says nothing. She looks at me out of the corner of her eye. She holds very still.

"You know," I say to the room at large, but mostly to Paige, "I missed you while I was gone. I really wanted to be here with you."

There's a weighted pause, and then:

"I don't believe you."

"You don't have to believe me, but I'm going to tell you anyway. I care about you so much, Paige. I missed you every second."

She holds herself stiffly away for another moment, and then Paige's resolve crumbles. Her stool wobbles behind her as she launches herself off of it and into my arms.

"I found a shell on the beach," Paige says around a mouthful of grilled cheese. "Part of it was broken. But then I found another one that was curly." She makes the curling motion with her finger. "And there were feathers."

"What color?"

Beau tips the frying pan into the sink along with the plate he was using to butter the bread. The distance between us now feels worse than when I was in Houston and he was here. I want to touch him. More than that I want him to touch me. He glances up from the sink, his expression unreadable, and my skin goes tight and hot.

"White," Paige says, scowling. "Beau wouldn't let me bring one back. He said it might have germs on it."

"It did have germs on it," Beau puts in, and his voice is gravelly with how tired he is. "You don't bring feathers into the house."

"Sometimes you do." Paige narrows her eyes. "Sometimes people do bring feathers inside. People make things from feathers."

"Sometimes they do," I agree, and her attention snaps back to me. Her shoulders relax. "The most important thing is to wash your hands when you come inside from the beach."

"I always wash my hands," Paige answers, and then she's off. I've only been gone for a few days but she talks to me like I've been gone for months. She talks to me like she's not sure I'll stay, which is heartbreaking but accurate. I'm not sure if I'll stay. It's possible nobody is ever sure about that kind of thing.

She says something to Beau, and he answers, and I don't hear what it is because I'm too busy peeking at him and pretending not to. Beau dries his hands on the towel by the sink, his eyes on me. Paige is looking, too. They're waiting for me to say something.

"Jane," insists Paige.

Beau lets go of the hand towel. "It's time for her bath."

"Yes. Of course it is."

"I want Jane." Paige crosses her arms over her chest, and Beau sighs. He keeps it quiet to hide it from Paige, but I see the slope of his shoulders and the weary circles under his eyes. I see how being gone put them at odds again.

"We'll head upstairs." This could be the moment Beau takes me to the door of the inn and locks it behind me. *You don't work for me anymore, Jane.* This is his chance to go against me, if he's going to. A muscle works in his jaw. He says nothing. "Bath—"

"Then bed," Paige says, and there's such relief in her voice that it makes me tear up a little.

I concentrate the hardest I ever have on shampooing her hair and listening to her stories about the bath toys and asking questions about the shells on the beach. It's hard, because Beau hovers nearby, not quite out of hearing distance but not close enough to touch. I can feel his presence on the second floor of the inn. I know he wants more than what I've given him. I know I want more than what he's given me. But first it's bath time, and then bed.

He comes back into Paige's room while we're reading a story. Her head rests on the pillow. She's already half-dozing as I finish the book and close it. Beau pulls up her covers, businesslike but affectionate, and then the two of us walk out into the hall. Paige's door clicks closed behind us.

The constrained man from the kitchen disappears, and Beau's hands are on me. He pulls me into his bedroom and palms the door closed, his hand resting just above my head. I'm backed against it. Cornered. Which means I can't back down.

I can't let him do this yet. I duck out from under his hand and find space in the center of the room.

"Why?" His voice is gruff, and relief flashes across his eyes. "Why did you come back?"

"To help."

His eyes search mine. "To help Paige?"

"In a way. And to help Emily."

Beau's shocked, his eyes wide. Was it true, what she said? Did she bring me here because he cares about me? "What?"

"She came to see me."

He blinks. "She's really alive, then."

"Yes, she's really alive. She came to my apartment in Houston, and we talked. About a lot of things. What she's been doing all this time. And about you. She's been living in her friend's cabin and hiding all this time."

Beau runs a hand through his hair, obviously worried about her. "Those places aren't insulated. You can't stay there for the winter."

"She didn't feel like she could access her money. It would just give her away."

"Em should have known better than that." *Em.* Hearing him use a nickname for her hurts. He sounds indignant, and concerned. He *cares* about her. It's written all over his face. The surprise in his eyes. My old fear from the plane feels cold and bitter. What if he loves her? What if he's still in love with her? "She should have known she could call me. Whatever she did—we could have sorted it out."

"She didn't think that was an option. That's why she came to talk to me."

His eyes narrow. He seems more dangerous than ever, in this small room. "Why didn't *you* call me?"

"Because I didn't need you." I ignore how good it feels to have him in my sight. I ignore the rapid shift in his breathing and the way he's blocking the door. I give him a cool look. "I can handle some things, you know. I'm not made of porcelain."

Beau knew it, too. He sent me away knowing I'd be able to take care of myself. He can't be surprised to find I've actually done it. His eyes rake down over me, as if he's expecting to find another person wearing my clothes and my face. "Where did she see you?" he demands.

"My apartment." It's hard to breathe when he looks like this. Handsome and domineering. It's like an ocean swell has crashed through the window. "She came to my apartment."

"When?" Beau doesn't raise his voice, but his tone is hard.

"As soon as I got back home."

"I called you." His eyes blaze. "I called you, and you said everything was fine."

"It was fine."

"It wasn't fine if a dead woman was standing in your apartment."

"Actually, she was sitting at first. At my desk. She sat there until she got up and pulled a gun on me." His hands flex at his sides and his whole body tenses. He looks me up and down, then again, scanning for something. Searching. "What are you doing?"

His eyes come up to mine, and I see that he's not furious—or that he is furious, but he's also worried. Horror is written in his face. "Goddamn it, Jane. You should have told me. That should have been the first thing out of your mouth."

It occurs to me that he's checking for bullet wounds. "She didn't shoot me," I insist. "And I wasn't going to walk in here and say that in front of Paige. What's important is that I believe what she said. She's telling the truth about what happened to her. Next time—"

"There won't be a next time," he growls. "You think you're walking out of here again? You're not."

I think he might lock me in here. Physically block the way out, he's so angry. He's not going to move out of the way until this is over. "It's not going to be like that."

"Like what?" The heat of him fills the room.

"You with all the power and me with nothing. I'm not here as a penniless employee who can be sent away at any moment."

Beau looks as torn as I've ever seen him look. "And I can't keep you here? I can't keep you safe?"

"No. Only I can do that."

Beau takes a step back, closing himself off

from me. He folds his arms across his chest, expression stormy. "Why did you come back, Jane?"

"Because Emily asked for my help. She's been in hiding since she saw Joe Causey kill Rhys, and she wanted my help. And she's Paige's mother."

"You believe her."

"I wouldn't have gotten on the plane otherwise."

This doesn't calm him. "Why the hell are you here if you won't let me protect you? Anything could have happened to you." His fear is barely disguised behind his anger. "Why would you bother coming back if I can't—"

"You have to give me the choice." He shakes his head at the interruption. Does he even know he's doing it? "I want to choose. I'm not the nanny you can send away whenever you're finished with me. And I'm not your prisoner. I belong to myself before I belong to you."

"Fine," he says through gritted teeth. "Fine, Jane. You belong to yourself. Is that what you want me to say? That you can leave? I don't want—" He swallows the rest of his sentence. "What do you want?"

"I'm choosing to be here. With you."

CHAPTER SIX

Jane Mendoza

"YOU'RE CHOOSING THIS." Beau's tone is almost sarcastic. Sharper than I've heard in a long time. It's worse than it was the night I arrived at Coach House. Back then, he didn't know me. He'd never claimed to care about me. Now he's done those things and more. "This."

"I'm not made of porcelain." I feel more breakable with him staring at me like this, but I stand my ground. Beau sent me away because he thought I would be safer away from him.

I came back because the danger is worth it.

I know it is. Or it will be, once things are settled. They can't be settled until Beau and I work this out. The tension in the room feels like a wire about to snap. It's wound up around my heart. It's like watching him fall off a cliff, only he's standing right in front of me.

"Oh?" He advances on me, the broad strength of him intimidating. My heart speeds up. But I keep my eyes on his. This is a challenge from Beau. I'm not sure I can win. Maybe he can break me, even if I tell him I'm not fragile. He could break my heart. My body.

My body definitely wants him, even though he pushed me away. There's so much heat between my thighs and wearing a bra is a small torture. I want his mouth on mine and his skin against mine. Even like this. Beau is so close we're sharing the same air. I can see the lightning flashes of anger in his eyes. He's taller, and so much stronger, so much more muscle.

If I fought him, I would lose. No question in my mind. I couldn't resist him. I couldn't push him away.

I don't want to fight him.

He's looking for signs that I do. Expecting them. I can see that in his eyes and in the way his mouth curves into the beginnings of a sneer. I stand up taller and let him do it. Yes, my heart is pounding. Yes, I would say that I was scared. I'm still not going to cower.

He puts a fist in my hair and drags me closer. The pain surprises me. I almost let a cry escape from my lips. No—I won't do it. This is a test.

He leans in so close I think he must be about to kiss me again. I want to taste his desperation. It would make us closer together, if he would let me have that. He must think kissing me before was a mistake. That it might have shown his hand.

He doesn't kiss me.

Beau bites me instead.

A new shock of pain reverberates through me. "What if I pushed you too far?" he murmurs against my bitten lips. "What if I demand too much? Would you stop me?"

My breath catches. I'm not sure if I would stop him. I don't know, I don't know. I want him too much. It makes my decisions hazy and hard to hold on to. The sensation of his hands on me and his eyes on me and his heat in this room makes it impossible to say what I'd do. Shameful, for a woman who should know better.

I don't know better than Beau Rochester.

A sound escapes him, like a laugh, and I see in his eyes that he's sensed my weakness and indecision. He turns me in his hands and pushes my face against the wall. I press my cheek against the rose-patterned wallpaper of the inn and try to breathe. Beau's hands are everywhere on me now. He's touching me everywhere, groping, rough. Hard squeezes on sensitive skin. My breasts. My belly. Everywhere he can reach. My breathing comes faster. With the wall hemming me in, I'm caught. It's the worst position to be in. The one I'm supposed to avoid at all costs.

I don't want to avoid him. My body responds to him, nipples tightening, slickness between my legs. He's testing me. This is a test to see if I'll break, or if I'll beg him to stop. Run out of the room, maybe. Run back to Houston. *Admit I'm the most dangerous person you've ever been with, and that I'm ruining your life.*

Beau's going to take what he wants, but he won't get everything. I won't admit that to him. It's not true, no matter how much he believes it.

He shoves a hand down my shirt and pinches one nipple hard enough to pull a pained sound out of me. "Enough?" he demands. "Say the word, sweetheart. Tell me to stop."

No. I'll be damned. I've survived worse to get to Beau Rochester in the first place, and I'm not going to give in. I press my lips closed. He lets out a frustrated growl and turns me to the bed. Bends me over it. He's rough taking my clothes off. Beau tears at the fabric in a way that's almost clinical. It burns as he yanks my shirt, my pants, everything away. I could be an object, or a doll, for all the care he takes undressing me. It's so hot it has me panting. So very, very wrong.

He pins me to the bed with one hand. The only move I can make is to turn my head to try to see his face. His eyes are dark. Pained. And distant. Like I could be anyone on this bed. Like he's just using me. "Enough?"

"No."

The first smack against my ass makes me gasp, and the second brings tears to my eyes. The third makes them spill over. He's not holding back at all. My feet kick up off the floor involuntarily. Beau stops only to feel between my legs. "You're wet for this," he says. "You like it mean."

On some level, I do. I do like this. It makes me feel strong, the way he doesn't have to be gentle with me. But it's harsh now. Meaner than he's ever been. He rains blows down on my ass like it was me who left him. A punishment for what he did to himself. What he did to us both. When he stops, my skin is fiery and my tears are just as hot.

Beau undoes his belt buckle and shoves his pants to the floor. There's nothing sweet in his touch when he moves me onto the bed. It's only to brace my knees and push my face down to position me for him.

"Look how much your cunt wants this," he

taunts, thrusting two fingers in, then adding a third. He twists them and I moan. "Look how much you want this."

"What about you?"

"I want this."

He takes his fingers out and pushes himself in. Beau's wild behind me, with no consideration for whether I'm ready, or whether I can take it. I am ready. And I can take it. Worst of all, I want it. I can feel myself clenching around him as he takes me. His motion drives me into the covers. I can't catch my breath. I can't slow my racing heart.

"Do you wish I would play with your clit and make you come? You look like you want that, too." I can't speak. He slaps my ass again and shoves in deeper. To the point of pain. "Do it yourself."

I don't know whether this is part of the test or not, but I think it is. I reach between my legs.

Beau curses, but he doesn't slow. I can't find any rhythm. The only pleasure I can feel right now is that he's close, and it's a painful one. He takes me with deep strokes, his hips meeting my body with violence. I don't need to touch myself. I just need him.

I reach back for his hand. Desperation presses at my lungs. I just want to connect with him, just need some sign that the man I love is in there, but he traps my hand against my body and holds it there.

This is how far I've fallen.

Bent over on this bed at the inn, my former boss behind me. My face in the covers. My ass in the air. It's a humiliating, degrading position and he doesn't care.

"You're tight," he says, and it sounds like he's gritting his teeth, sounds like he's putting everything into fucking me. "You're a good fuck, Jane. Tight on my cock. I could come like this."

I can't get any lower. He's being cruel and rough and terrible. Beau's trying his best to push me away, and he's succeeding. He's inside me but it feels like there are miles between us. His heart is completely closed off to me. His emotions. There's only this physical, animal thing.

"Enough?" he asks again.

It's barely a word, he's fucking me so hard. Run, his tone says. Push me away from you and go back to a life without me. Prove to me that what we had was nothing and you know better than to fall for me.

He's expecting me to say that it's too much. That he's too much, that all this pain is too much, that all the things he's ever done are too much to live with. If I said that, he would stop. He'd leave the room and never touch me again. I'd never see his dark eyes light up when I entered a room again. Beau Rochester would be over for me.

But he can never be over for me. He already owns my heart. He just doesn't know it. He doesn't trust it, and that breaks my heart.

The scent of him is in every breath I take. I can feel his muscles working behind me and the forceful grip of his hands. I wanted to taste his desperate kiss again, but it's in his body now, in every move he makes. It's not going to work. I need him too much.

It's a struggle to catch my breath enough to answer him. "No." My voice trembles with the force of his thrusts. "Not enough."

When would it ever be enough? Never. Not for as long as I live. I don't know where I got the idea that I wouldn't be enough for him. He's more than enough for both of us, even at his most broken.

He's never been this rough with me. Beau's pushing me to the limit, trying to force me beyond it so I have to admit defeat. He works himself in deeper and holds my hips tight so I can't get away from the invasion of him. I roll against him, trying to get more contact. Anything

I can get. I'm not above begging for scraps of his affection right now. I'm not above anything. He's the worst he's ever been.

Despite that, I want him.

Even now.

CHAPTER SEVEN

Beau

IT'S HELL, HAVING her struggle against me like this. Not because it doesn't feel good. It feels so damn good. I've never felt anything this good in my life, and I'm being a nightmare. Jane takes the covers in her fists and circles her hips. She doesn't have anywhere to go. I'm holding her too tight. She keeps on trying, driving back against me.

I made her touch herself because I knew that if I did it, I'd give in to her. There's a part of me that wants to, and another part that knows I should run her out of town. She got here safe. That doesn't mean she is safe.

Jane lets out a whimper. "Please," she says.

That one word out of her mouth tears something free from around my heart. It's too hard to maintain this distance between us. It's like a heart attack. I've pushed lots of women away by being an asshole and I can't do it anymore. I can't. Even if it's best for her.

I run a hand around her hips and slide it down until I find her clit. Jane shivers. I'm not going to be nice. It doesn't matter. She wants it, even this rough, demanding touch. She tries and tries to angle her hips into my fingertips.

"Is this enough for you?"

"No," she whispers, but I don't take my fingers away. I'm past it now. I have to keep touching her. This is what I was trying to hold myself back from. She's an addiction, and she's the kind that makes a man weak. Weak as hell. Her fists clench on the covers and her hips go still, pushing back against mine.

That's all it takes.

Me, touching her. Jane comes, and the sound she makes is so beautiful. The way she shakes and flutters around me is so beautiful and soft and trusting. No part of her tries to pull away.

My resolve crumbles under the weight of her need. I run my hands over her lower back. Over the handprint I left on her ass. I never thought I would be this man again. Needing a woman. Caring about her. Risking my goddamn heart. But here I am. Guilt comes next, for being so rough with her. The handprint—Jesus. I don't normally play this part. The sadistic asshole billionaire who doesn't give a damn.

I turn her over and pull her upright. Jane blinks at me, her dark eyes wide. "Make me pay for that." It's as demanding as anything else I've said tonight. "Punish me back."

She still has tears in her eyes, and she wipes them away with a flick of her fingers. Then she points toward the pillow. "There."

I lie back against it. Jane takes a minute to compose herself, breathing deep and steady. My cock throbs. It kills me, looking at her like this. She's so goddamn beautiful. Slightly shaken from her orgasm and from the ordeal of being with me. I'd give anything for her to touch me, but she waits until my cock twitches. A smile flickers across her face, and it's the most wicked I've ever seen her.

She crawls over me and hooks her nails into my abs. Drags them down. Refuses to touch me. I can't stop the grunt that comes out of me. I want her hands on my cock. I want her to ride me. I want her payback more.

Jane drags a fingertip around the base of my cock, still not touching me. She does it again. I deserve this. Her eyes on my face are the hottest thing and the most violating. Goose bumps run up the length of my body. Slowly, so slowly I'm probably going to have a heart attack, she lowers her head. The ends of her hair brush against my skin first, and then—

Her lips.

She takes them away as soon as they meet the stretched-tight head of my cock. "You have to wait," she says. Her voice is nothing like I would say it. If it weren't for the glint in her eyes, I would think she felt sorry for me. Empathetic to the last.

"I'll wait."

Jane leans back in and licks around my tip. Her tongue is so soft it makes my toes curl. She watches me with luminous eyes, tracking every tensing muscle and involuntary sound. I make another one when she takes some of me into her mouth. More when she licks along the underside of me, along a sensitive vein.

She drags it out.

"This?" she keeps asking. "This?" And her tongue does terrible things to me. It makes me into a mindless fool. It makes me into nothing but a bundle of nerves and pent-up desire. Jane takes me into her mouth as deep as she can, testing the different ways she can hold her tongue against me. My God, I thought she was gone forever. I thought I would never see her again. I deserve this torture.

She wraps her hands around me and works at it. Muscles fire, one after the other. Jane takes her mouth away and peers up at me, scolding. "You have to wait," she says again. "I told you to wait."

"Fuck."

Just when it can't get worse, she reaches for my hand again. This time, I give it to her. She puts it in her hair, her other hand still wrapped around me. "Hmm," she says, the tip still in her mouth. That sound goes all the way to my spine. To my heart. Jane lifts her mouth away. "That's what you like."

Yes. I might not try to be an asshole every waking moment, but touching her like this—touching her like I might fuck her mouth, and tell her how to do it—it makes me harder. That shouldn't be possible. It happens anyway. Jane puts her hand over mine and pleasure darkens the edges of my vision. She's still in control of this. I never knew it could be so hot. I never knew I'd like it so damn much this way.

Jane gives a little over to me, letting me push her down onto me again and again in the steady rhythm I want. She takes me deep, the head of me meeting the back of her throat. And then she swallows.

I almost come up off the bed, it feels so good. Jane gives me a last, long lick and I realize what she's doing the second before it happens.

She sits back on her heels and looks down at me. My heart races. My free hand is braced against the wall like the wall can help me. I've never been this hard in my life. And Jane just watches. She looks at me, caught here by her. I asked her for this. I got what I wanted. I can't breathe. My brain is frantic for anything she can give me. My thoughts latch on to how perfect she looks, naked and tousled and here.

I don't know what I was thinking before, trying to push her away. I guess I wanted proof that she wouldn't leave. Goddamn it, she came back here with Emily. That's proof enough.

Jane shifts her weight, her eyes moving along a path from my cock to my eyes. Does she know what she looks like right now? A miracle. She catches me looking and inches her knees apart so I can see between her legs. It's mostly shadow and glistening flesh. She might be punishing me, but she's waiting, too. Her lips part like she might say something, but then she shakes her head. Nothing.

"Jane."

She cocks her head to the side and her hair brushing her shoulder almost makes me come on my own stomach.

"It hurts," I admit. It really does. It hurts to be this hard. Hurts more than I can explain. The hurt rises through my abs to my chest. I'm one long chain of need for Jane Mendoza.

Jane nods, silent. Waiting.

Enough, I want to say. Enough. I learned my lesson. I fucking get it. I'll never let you walk out of here again. I'll drag you into this mess with me even if it's not right for you. A perfect woman deserves a perfect life, not Beau Rochester, not damaged goods. But it's not enough. I'll spend every day from now until the end hurting just like this if that's what it takes to keep her with me.

The last bit of my resistance can't match her eyes on mine. I want her too much. I was too worried, every second she was gone. I'm going to die if I don't come.

"Please."

Her eyes light up at this pathetic, grunted please, and Jane crawls over to me like a cat. This time, she's not testing. She takes me into her mouth, and my vision darkens. There's only the wet heat of her mouth and the pressure of her tongue and the hold she has on me. Demanding as all hell. My orgasm is like a bomb. It lights up every muscle, head to toe, and makes my heart skip a beat. Several beats. Jane swallows furiously, trying to keep up, which only makes me come harder. My toes dig into the bed.

She stays where she is until it's over.

CHAPTER EIGHT

Beau Rochester

EMILY'S STAYING AT a friend's cabin in the forest on the other side of town.

Mateo drives. I sit in the passenger seat and tally up the months she spent there, barely a hundred miles from her daughter. It must have killed her to be that close. That pain must have gotten to her in the end, if it sent her creeping over the cliffside at night. We pull off the main road and onto a private two-track road that's all gravel and ruts. Trees close in behind us in moments. It's a good place to hide, if you don't want to be found. In the driver's seat Mateo is silent and thoughtful.

The A-frame is so small you could blink and miss it. Mateo's already at a crawl from the potholes, so it's an easy turn to park the car next to one I don't recognize. Too cheap to be a rental.

The curtains over the front windows are drawn tight, but as we get out of the car, one of them flickers.

"This place isn't built for winters," Mateo says, almost to himself. He's right. There's no room in the structure for insulation. Birds call in the clearing. Their travels have been uninterrupted by our arrival. My heart twists up into a knot. I'd rather be in bed with Jane, or hell, even trying to bargain with Paige until she does her homework.

"No," I agree. "Let's get this over with."

The two of us go up to the door and knock. It opens instantly and there she is.

Emily Rochester, my brother's wife, died and come back again. "Beau," she says, but then her eyes narrow with suspicion as they slide to Mateo. "You brought a friend."

"We've met before." Mateo sticks out his hand to shake and Emily flinches back. A subtle movement, covered by the lift of her chin. "Mateo Garza."

The two of them shake, then Emily steps back into the half-light of the A-frame. "I'd rather not talk with the door open."

She checks outside once, then twice, before she closes the door and turns back to us. Emily's as beautiful as she always was, but she's different. There's a new wariness in her eyes. Suspicion in the set of her lips. Nothing like the girl I fell in love with all those years ago. To be honest, I expected some of that emotion to come back when I saw her again like this, face to face, but now…

It's not nothing, what I feel. But it's not the painful obsession I felt when I first met her, before she got together with Rhys. That belongs to someone else now.

That belongs to Jane Mendoza.

There's a moment of heavy silence. It's so goddamn tiring, all of this. Thinking she was dead. Finding out she was alive. Sending Jane away. Getting her back. And I still don't understand, so we'll start there.

"What the hell happened, Em?"

"My brother's a dirty cop." Her lips tremble. "You always said I spoiled him."

"Don't blame yourself. Whatever he did is on him."

"Bribes. Stolen property. Money laundering. I found out the night he died."

"The night he killed Rhys."

She flinches. "Yes. I saw them arguing. Joe didn't know I was there. He didn't know I watched him shoot my husband until I screamed."

I curse, thinking of how close she came to death that night. "Hell."

"Why didn't you come to me? I would have helped you."

She shifts her weight from foot to foot, her expression softening at my tone. "Rhys is your brother. I didn't think you'd believe me. You might even have blamed me—"

"I know what he was like."

Mateo sticks his hands in his pockets. "You're just going to believe her? Whatever she says?"

Emily glances at him, but Mateo keeps his focus on me. This isn't how I want the conversation to go. He's bristling, obviously suspicious of Emily. Obviously pissed, and I'm not having a separate discussion with him about why.

Mateo's had front-row seats to the aftermath of losing Emily and Rhys. He should have said something on the way over if it was still bothering him this much, but now we're here, and—

"Yes. I do." I like to think that I would have believed her if she'd come to me before. But I definitely believe her now that she's come with Jane on her side. For better or for worse, I trust Jane. And she believes this. So I do, too.

Besides, Emily's here in this bare-bones A-frame with hardly any furniture that must have been cold as hell in the winter and she's alive. Emily was the only one on that boat with my brother and Joe Causey. I'll never hear what she has to say if Mateo keeps being an asshat. I put out my hand in the universal gesture for *take it fucking easy* and turn back to Emily.

"I'm here to listen to you. I want to know what happened."

It's more than a want. It's a need. I need to know what possessed her to hide out here for months. I need to know what made her follow Jane to Houston. I need to know everything. I've spent these months completely out of my depth, and I need answers.

Emily glares at Mateo for another few beats, then releases a breath. She pushes away from the door and brushes past me on her way into the house. It might not have anything beyond a chair and a ratty rug, but Emily plants her feet in the center of it like it's Coach House and runs a hand through her hair. "I've always protected Joe." She gives an unsteady laugh. "You complained about it when we were going out, but I never understood how you could be too protective, too loyal. We grew up without anyone but each other."

Mateo looks like he wants to give her shit, but I shoot him a glare.

"It was supposed to be a dinner out on the water."

"You hate boats."

That earns me a wan smile. "But Rhys liked them. And, by that time, I'd learned to do whatever it took to keep him happy. It was about survival."

A pang of guilt slashes my insides. How could my brother have been a monster? Why didn't I know? But I guess Emily's dealing with the same shock over her own brother.

"Joe showed up. He started fighting with Rhys. I watched him kill my husband." Her voice breaks. "There was no love between us, but he didn't deserve to die. Not over money. Joe didn't know I was there, but I couldn't help it—I screamed."

Cold runs down my spine. She may not have died that night, but she came close.

"He thought I would protect him. There was no doubt in his mind about it. He talked about how we'd take the boat out and dump Rhys's body, how I'd call the Coast Guard and say there was an accident, how no one would doubt the story."

"You told him no." We might not have been made for each other, but I know her. She may have spoiled her little brother, but she would never condone murder.

Not even if the bastard deserved it. Too bad Joe Causey didn't end Rhys for the right reasons—protecting his sister the way she protected him.

No, I could already see the way this played out.

"He said Rhys was stealing from him, that he deserved it." Tears in her eyes. "I didn't even understand what he meant. How could Rhys steal from him? That was when he told me about the bribes. And the drugs. All the ways he was a dirty cop."

"And Rhys helped him." Christ. My brother was more evil than I knew.

"They laundered money through some real estate investments Rhys made. Apparently that's why Joe needed him. It would have raised red flags if he'd owned that much property."

Anger flows through me. Rhys had been an angry child. Apparently he'd grown into a worse man. The knowledge doesn't sit well, considering I'd left Emily to him. Along with Paige. "Joe thought you'd continue protecting him."

"I couldn't even pretend or act the part. I was shaking from head to toe. You could see it in his eyes, the moment he realized I might tell someone what I saw. The decision he made to get rid of me. He told me we were going to dump his body in the ocean, but he meant me, too. So I waited until he went below to get rope, and then I jumped overboard and swam away."

Christ. Thinking of her at night in the ocean. She's not a strong swimmer. "You could have died."

She gives me a small, sad smile. "Sometimes it feels like I did." Her gaze goes distant for a moment. Imagining her death, maybe. "You know Debbie Harris?"

The name rings a vague bell. Auburn hair, I think. Kind eyes. "Does she work at the hospital?"

"Sometimes. She's a traveling nurse, so she's not here very often. Two years behind us in school. She said I could stay, so I stayed. I thought I would keep my head down and wait for something to happen."

"Wait for what?" Mateo asks, his tone biting.

"I don't know," Emily fires back. "I don't know. Maybe I was waiting for Joe to fuck up so badly the rest of the police force would notice. But that never happens. They protect their own."

Her laugh is bitter and sad. "What was I going to do, walk into the station and tell them he'd tried to kill me? They'd think I was crazy, and then I'd never have a chance to get Paige back."

Her voice cracks on Paige's name, and that's it. That's what made her do all this shit. She wants Paige back. "You could have come to me."

Emily's eyes shine with tears. "No, I couldn't have. What if Joe had discovered me? How would it be better to get killed in front of Paige? I had to stay out of sight."

"But you didn't," Mateo points out. "You stalked them. And then you followed Jane to Houston."

"With a goddamn gun," I say, because I'm not going to forgive that so easily. I believe that Emily's telling the truth, but the thought of a bullet in Jane's body makes me see red.

"Yeah. I did. And maybe it wasn't a good plan, but you're here." Emily looks back at me. "I miss Paige so much that it hurts to breathe. Every day—" Her hands go to her chest. "I miss her. I want her to be with me. If we can fix all this, I want her to be with me."

I have the same sensation I did when I slid down the cliff, only my leg doesn't break on impact. It's worse. Because what this means is that

I'm going to lose Paige. It's been so goddamn difficult, trying to figure things out with her, trying not to fuck it all up. But what Emily's suggesting is an end to all that. A return to the way it was before.

Except there is no going back to how it was before.

"I'll help you," I say, my voice tight. "I'll help you, and Jane will help you, but you're not going to get Paige back. Not right away. We have to make sure you aren't in danger first. No more watching us. No more haunting the beach at night."

"If there was any hope of even seeing Paige again, I had to—" She looks down at the floor. "I didn't have to do that. I regret it. I just want my daughter. You have—" She's choked up. Struggling. "You have to understand that."

Emily doesn't take her eyes off me, and Mateo's watching her like he's a human lie-detector test. And according to his expression, she's failing.

"Well," he says. "You got us here. What's your new plan, Emily? What do you have in mind to fix all this?" The skepticism in his tone verges on derision, but there's something more complicated in his eyes. No idea what.

"I need help." Emily's hands fall to her sides, hanging uselessly.

It feels wrong to see her like this. Rattling around a barely furnished cabin in the woods. Defeated and begging for help. It never would have gotten this far if I'd listened to her back then. If I'd done something about Rhys back then. I should have. I know that. But my long history with my brother clouded my judgment. I knew what it would mean to pick a fight with him. Rhys didn't lose fights, and she'd chosen him, but none of that excuses my inaction. "Nobody's going to believe me if I speak against Joe. They'd believe you, though."

"The police department isn't going to listen to a word I say."

"But you can go above the police department." Hope has come back into Emily's eyes. It must hurt like hell. I can see that it does. She looks like I felt when Jane was gone. Fucking wretched. And she's been separated from Paige for months.

"In a place like this, there isn't anybody above the police." Mateo's not buying any of this. He crosses his arms over his chest and looks at me expectantly. I'm supposed to be the one to shut this down now and kill the hope in Emily's eyes.

"There are a few people I could talk to." Mateo scoffs. Emily holds her breath. "But it's not a guarantee. I don't know how this all shakes out."

"But you'll try?"

Leaves rustle outside the cabin as the breeze picks up. It almost sounds like rain, but there's not a cloud in the sky today. Jane and Paige will be on the strip of beach by the inn or walking in the yard with the sun in their hair. I want to be with them, and strangely enough, I want Emily to not be in this murky piece-of-shit house. Not because I want her with me. Only because I know how happy it would make Paige. She's missed her mother just as desperately as Emily has missed her.

As much as I'll miss her when all of this is said and done.

If I can fix it.

"I'll try," I promise her. It's a shitty promise to have to make. If I succeed, it means carving out parts of my own life and handing them back to the world. Back to Emily. It means giving Paige back to Emily, and after that—I don't know what else. Mateo sighs. "I'll try."

CHAPTER NINE

Emily Rochester

IT WEARS ON the soul, being dead. Having to cut your hair and wear sunglasses. Having to look away when you pass someone on the street. Having no phone or email or connection in the world. Even Facebook thinks I'm dead.

There were times I *felt* dead, as if I really did drown in the ocean. Maybe only the ghost of Emily Rochester climbed onto the frozen rocks, gasping for air.

Now I've been thrust into the land of the living. I'm painfully alive.

"Just…give me a minute. Okay?" Beau asks.

"Okay." He can take as long as he wants, if he's going to help me fix this.

Beau steps outside with his phone. That leaves me in the cabin… with Mateo.

"Interesting."

Mateo Garza was hot in high school. All the girls wanted to be with him, but I wasn't interested in a player. I only had eyes for Beau.

After an unmoored home life, I wanted safety. Security.

A laughable goal considering what happened.

"What's interesting?" I say, my voice flat. I don't want to engage with him. It's clear he's skeptical of me. No, worse than that. He's outright distrustful.

"That you didn't reach out to Beau sooner. Or me, for that matter."

A startled laugh escapes me. "You? For all I knew you would turn me over to the police. After finding out my brother was a dirty cop and my husband was helping him, I couldn't trust anyone."

More skepticism. "Interesting that you left your daughter behind."

Pain steals my breath. It's been torture to be away from Paige. She's my heart, walking around, eating, sleeping. "I protected her the only way I could. She would have been in danger on the run. I was a moving target. I became a target the moment Joe pulled the trigger."

"You didn't trust Beau enough to turn to him. But you left Paige with him?"

"Beau had no reason to hurt her. I didn't think he'd believe me, but I also didn't think he'd harm an innocent child. God, even Rhys never hit her." As soon as the words are out of my mouth, I know I've made a mistake. I've said too much.

Awareness darkens Mateo's eyes. "But he hit you, didn't he?"

"That's none of your business. Why are you even here?"

"Because I'm Beau's friend. Someone he can trust. Someone who didn't betray him."

"I never betrayed him." There's a stab of pain at my breastbone, because I did hurt him. And he hurt me. Maybe that's all that love has to offer—pain. "And I never cheated on him. He's the one who left me."

"To make his way in the world."

"And he couldn't bring me with him?"

"Would you have liked that? The parties in LA? The drugs? The clubs?"

"I have no idea."

"I think you would have. I think you're just ambitious enough to have found some older, richer sugar daddy. Someone who could give you a Beverly Hills mansion and a boob job."

"How dare you."

"Lucky for him, you picked the other brother.

Is that why Beau is still alive?"

Breath catches in my throat. "You think I killed Rhys?"

"You wouldn't be the first woman who's been knocked around to decide she's had enough. And he had some money, didn't he? He made you a rich widow."

I'm surprised by how much it hurts, his accusation. He's no one to me. He's nothing. At least that's what I tell myself. Instead it twists my heart. "This is why I couldn't call you. Or Beau. Because you're all the same, when it comes down to it. The world is a big, fat boys club."

Mateo stands, and I shy away from him. But he keeps coming, advancing, moving into my space until I'm backed against the wall. "Rhys Rochester was a piece of shit. And so's Joe Causey. It doesn't surprise me that they worked together. What surprises me is that you protected them."

"I didn't know what they were doing," I whisper.

This close I can see the golden flecks in his dark eyes. I can see the faint smile lines around his eyes. This is a face that's graced magazines in supermarkets. He's inches away from me. "You didn't know? Or you didn't want to know?"

"For someone just trying to survive, those are

the same thing."

His gaze drops to my lips. He reaches up a hand—to touch them? Or to slap me? The instinct runs too deep. It's been engraved into my skin. I flinch away from him. His hand hovers in the air, frozen. "He really did a number on you, didn't he?"

I learned to protect myself from men's fists before Rhys. "Don't pretend like you care."

He moves slower now, more careful. He puts his hand on my cheek. His thumb sweeps back and forth, sending goose bumps across my skin. "You should have reached out to me."

"I thought you'd be busy. With parties. And drugs. And clubs."

"Those things aren't as fun as they look."

My lips twitch. "Liar."

"Fine. They're pretty fun." His thumb stops on my lips. And taps. Every nerve ending becomes electric. I feel the soft pressure of his thumb everywhere in my body. "I would have helped you."

"Liar," I say again, though it's less funny this time. "You would have been loyal to Beau."

"Yes, but I don't think I need to choose between you two. Not now, anyway."

"What does that mean—not now?"

"It means I had a crush on Emily Marie Causey. The whole school knew it. Even Beau figured it out. Only you seemed oblivious to that fact. You only wanted Beau."

I search the shadows of memory—the nights I spent at bonfires and keggers so I wouldn't have to go home. Getting in between my father and Joe, because they were always fighting. And fights meant fists. Beau had seemed like the golden boy. A path to stability. Mateo represented everything I didn't trust—emotion and risk and drama. He'd flirted with me, but he'd also flirted with every girl in school. Some of the boys, too. "You're making that up."

He shakes his head, slow and certain, never breaking eye contact. "I would go to bed at night and dream about how you'd taste. I thought I'd never get to find out."

That's the only warning I get. The only warning I get before he leans close. His lips replace his thumb, and I startle at the change. It's been so long since I've been kissed. And longer, since I actually enjoyed the sensation. At the end, with Rhys, it was about survival.

I would have endured anything for one more day with my daughter, and I did, I did. I endured everything which carried me to this moment—to

Mateo Garza brushing his lips against mine, teasing glances meant to lure me closer, meant to make me trust him. Doesn't he know I can't trust anyone?

There's no such thing as sex for me. No such thing as love.

There's only my daughter and the relentless drive to keep her safe.

The temptation of warmth pulls at my bones. It makes me ache, but I force him away, panting with the force it took to reject comfort. All I want is the safe haven of strong arms, but I've learned the hard way how much it hurts when those same arms lash out. "No," I say. "I can't."

He pulls back. Emotions cross his handsome face—surprise, curiosity, and a determination that makes my hackles rise. "You're right. Now's not the right time."

"There will *never* be a right time."

Before he can respond, Beau comes back inside, looking windswept. "I reached out to some people. They're going to get started with the information we have so far. But they'll need more. Witness statements. Corroboration." His gaze narrows on me. "They need to question you."

A shiver wracks me. I cross my arms in front of me, but I'm still cold. Nothing compares to the warmth of being held by Mateo. "Of course. I'll do it."

Anything for Paige. I didn't come this far only to falter now. Even if I can feel a dark gaze on me, assessing, as if seeking out the weak points in a fortress. I have to stay strong.

No matter how safe it felt in his arms.

CHAPTER TEN

Jane Mendoza

THE SHEET ON the bed curves over Beau's hips, just below the ridges of his abs. I trace this curve, and those ridges, with a fingertip. Charting the course between muscles. He breathes deeply now. Even. It's relaxation, even if only a brief respite.

He's here with me, in this room made warmer from the heat of our bodies.

Waves beat at the shore outside. One after the other, relentless, like all the doubts I have.

My imagination ran wild this morning. He and Mateo drove off together. When they came back, they were arguing in low, intense voices. It makes me think whatever happened with Emily was equally as intense. What did he do when he saw her for the first time after all this time? After believing she was dead? Did his eyes flash the way they did when he looked at me? Was his face broken open with relief?

Probably. It's naive to think he doesn't want her. When all of this is over, when everything is back to the way it should be, he'll want her then, too.

It just makes sense. Beau and Emily and Paige are the perfect family.

Emily's distraught right now because she misses Paige so much, because she's out of her mind with a mother's panic, but she fits better with him than I do. She's not some Houston transplant pretending to belong. She actually does belong, with her daughter and the man she loved.

The man she might *still* love, even if she denies it.

How could she not still be in love with him? His skin is warm, body solid beneath my cheek. Every heartbeat sounds like a secret. Any woman would crave this.

And honestly, she probably deserves him more than me. She survived so much to get here. She was courageous and bold and strong, and people like that deserve men like Beau.

All I did was accept a job.

Maybe that's why I gave in to the woman holding a gun. Not out of self-preservation. Not out of a desire to help Paige's mother. For the simple chance to see Beau again.

He tugs his fingers through my hair. "I can hear you thinking," he says.

It was easier not to think when he was between my legs ten minutes ago. It was harder to stay quiet. He put a big hand over my mouth to stifle the sounds I made.

Now it's loud in my head. "I'm wondering…"

I'm wondering how you felt when you first saw Emily this morning. Did you touch her the way you touched me? Did you kiss her to be sure she was real?

"Nothing."

"Hell." The admonishment sends heat through all of my limbs.

Heat to the tips of my fingers. "I'm wondering what you and Mateo talked about."

I'm not his nanny anymore, not his employee, but this still seems like a safer question than asking how he feels about Emily. I'm not sure I can survive it without my heart breaking.

"He doesn't trust Emily. Doesn't think I should believe her."

My heart races. That doesn't sound good. "Why not?"

He runs his hand over my hair and down to

my back. "He saw how hard it was with Paige. At the beginning. Hell, you saw it, too. I was in over my head. I was a goddamn wreck, and Paige deserved better. I think this is his way of trying to protect me."

"Do you believe her?"

He's quiet long enough that I realize I'm holding my breath. "Yes. I believe her." A short laugh. "It's too fucking insane to be made up."

"So you're going to help her."

"Yes. She's carried the burden alone for long enough."

Fear overwhelms me. I'm supposed to be standing on my own two feet right now, here only for Emily and Paige, but I need this for myself. "Is that why you're sad?"

"Sad?"

I put my hand over his heart. His chest is covered with rough hair. Warm skin. Beneath his breastbone, though, his heart beats. It's a gentle throb. "Sad."

His chest rises. Falls. "What do I have to be sad about?"

"You almost lost her."

Beau takes my chin in his hand and tips my face to his. He studies me for a long time, then leans down for a kiss. His lips brush mine—once, twice. Featherlight and almost nonexistent. It feels like a goodbye kiss. It feels like he's made a decision, and the only thing left to do is tell me what it is. "You think I'm sad because I almost lost Emily?"

"The two of you have history together." In comparison, I have nothing. A few months. They had years to miss each other and want each other and now there's nothing standing in the way. "Maybe you… Maybe you didn't even realize how much you missed her."

"I missed you." He's gruff about it. Sharp. Every word stabbing the air. "Every second you were gone felt like a goddamn year. You're the one I missed, Jane."

The words soothe a jagged place inside me. Still… "You can miss more than one person at the same time. You have so much in common. You match. I understand that."

"Christ. I went to that goddamn cabin today, and all I could think about, all I wanted was to come back to you. To hold you again. To make sure you didn't leave."

"Today you wanted that. What happens if Paige goes with her mother?" I can't trust that he'll still want me in a month. A year. I can't trust permanence when I've lived a temporary life.

"Would you still want me if I'm not the nanny?"

He looks incredulous. And fierce. "Would you still want me if I'm not Paige's guardian?"

"It's not the same thing."

"Isn't it?" He props himself on his arm. His eyes are dark pools above me. "We're both losing our identities. You think I don't see the way this plays out? If we put Joe away, if Emily can come out of hiding, then Paige will go back with her. We're both losing that little girl, and yes, hell yes, it makes me *sad*, but I'm sure as hell not going to lose you, too."

"I'm not yours." The denial is automatic. It's flimsy considering I'm naked in his bed right now, but my heart needs all the protection it can get.

Challenge sparks in his eyes. "No?"

My cheeks heat. He made me come so hard I was moaning his name, begging for him to stop. The echoes of my pleas remain in the room. "No."

He touches a hand to my side, beneath my breast. There's a small mole. "I missed this." He slides his hand down to my belly button. "And this." Lower, to the inside of my thigh, a place that's not specifically sexy but somehow even more intimate. Everything he's doing is intimate.

It tears down my defenses. "I missed every goddamn inch of you."

It's hard to explain how painful it was when he sent me away. Impossible to describe how it feels to be left behind—alone. Always alone. "It hurt."

Two words.

A lifetime of loneliness.

He drops his head. His forehead rests against the top curve of my breast. It's more personal than sex, what we're doing now. Linking our bodies together. Tying our hearts. "I tried to keep you safe, damn you. But here you are. In danger, and damned if that will stop me again."

"You won't send me away?"

"No, God help you. Though in the end, you may wish I did."

CHAPTER ELEVEN

Beau Rochester

Jane sleeps on the pillow, her dark hair sprawled across the white, and I'm awake.

My body is sated from what we've done, but I want more.

Will I always want more?

Yes, the ocean whispers outside. I will always want more the way the waves always want to run up on the sand. The water crushes boulders into fine grains over and over and over. It can never get enough of the shore. I'll never get enough of Jane.

How could I have ever thought of sending her away? I did worse than think of it. I did it. I made her leave when she didn't want to. Paige didn't want her to go. I didn't want her to go. Watching her car disappear from view was like being held underwater. Having her back is like breaking the surface after weeks of drowning.

She's oxygen.

I can breathe, and think. It's never been more clear how disastrous I am for women. Jane's done her best with me. She left when I told her to go and came back with her head held high, but it's not good for a person. It's not good for a woman to rely on my love for her. Love shouldn't be painful, and it is. Coming back hurt her. I know it did. I know it from the worry in her voice when she talks about Emily and the way she always seems braced for me to send her away again.

As if I could.

It would be better for her in the end if I did. I'm never good for women. Look at Emily. Look at Jane, frowning softly in her sleep.

The fact that I'm in bed with her at all should be proof enough that I'm terrible for her. A responsible boss doesn't get involved with the nanny. He doesn't dream of the scent of her skin. He doesn't lie awake at night watching her breathe. He doesn't let her back into the house after he does the right thing and sends her away.

Turns out I'm not a responsible boss, just like I haven't been a good man.

Claws scratch at the door. I get up and let Kitten in. She jumps up onto the bed and curls into a place next to Jane. I get back in the bed.

Jane stirs. She rolls over onto her back in the moonlight and blinks up at me. "You're awake," she says. "Why are you awake?"

The guarded expression sends another pang through my heart. I hurt her more than she's letting on when I sent her away, and now I've compounded the issue by not convincing her that I have no interest in being with Emily. It's always been my fear that I'll fuck things up beyond repair with a woman, and now that prophecy is coming true. "I couldn't sleep. Too much on my mind."

She swallows. "Are you thinking about Emily?"

"I was thinking about you." Not entirely true. "And I was trying to figure out what the hell to do about Emily." Jane tenses, but she doesn't speak. "At her place today, she wanted me to go above the police department. Above her brother."

Jane wrinkles her nose. "Who's above the police department?"

"Local prosecutor," I say. "I know her from school."

"Did you have classes together?"

"She had a crush on me. I never dated her because I was too interested in Emily."

Jane looks away. "You think she'll help you

now?"

"I think if Joe Causey gets to her first about this whole situation, none of us has a shot. But I could go to her. Talk to her about what's happened."

"Dazzle her with how rich and powerful you are?"

I stare down at her, wishing there was a way to understand her the way I do when I'm inside her. "I think it has less to do with being rich and powerful and more to do with having a history here. I've never been a white knight but I wasn't a complete asshole like Rhys. She'll have a conversation with me."

"What are you going to say?" Jane's dark eyes come back to mine and she tugs the sheet up higher on her chest. I want to pull it off her, expose all her skin and lick my way down and write the only thing that matters on her skin. Y O U C A M E B A C K. "Are you going to stand up for Emily?"

Another wave of guilt comes in. Another. Another. They're ceaseless. "I owe her that much. I should have done it years ago, and I didn't."

Jane searches my face. "What would you have done? Run away with her?"

I considered it. Of course I did. After the

night she came to me, after I fucked her to get revenge on Rhys, I went over a hundred different scenarios in my mind. Showing up at Coach House and dragging her out of there. Meeting her at an old dock on the beach. A runaway boat. A runaway train. But the thing about running is that eventually you have to stop. You can't outrun the past forever. It always catches up.

"Something different from what I did," I say finally. "Something other than turn my back on her. I always told myself I ran out of time, because Paige was born and the years went by."

"But you didn't run out of time," Jane says softly. "You could still…be with her. If you wanted it."

No. I don't want it. My heart knows first, body a second later. There's no going back with me and Emily. Hell, we might not have made it in the first place. What I felt for her was a teenage obsession. Everything seems fated in high school. Every emotion is heightened by raging hormones and, in my case, competition with Rhys. He hated that I was with Emily and that made me want her more. He's dead now. It doesn't feel like a victory. He was a piece of shit, bad for Emily and bad for Paige, but I didn't want her to lose her dad. Of all the things I planned, I never thought of outliving him and swooping in to take his place. I've always wanted my own place. Away from his shadow. Away from all of his cruelty and his dark obsession.

"You know what I felt when I saw Emily today?"

Jane shakes her head, wordless.

"Pity."

She lets out a breath. I'm not sure she knew she was holding it.

"I felt bad for her. This situation with Paige, and hiding out, and running after you to Houston in some desperate attempt to ask for help—it's fucked up. It's not what she ever wanted out of her life. She wanted a rich husband and a nice house and peace, and the world handed her a brother who didn't want to let her have it and a husband who didn't care. The place doesn't even have heat."

"What?"

"It's a summer cabin. Not meant for the winter." I can't go back and intervene on Emily's behalf. Never straighten things out between the two of us. And maybe there's a reason for that. Maybe it never worked out with Emily because I was supposed to meet Jane Mendoza instead. I don't believe in destiny or any of that bullshit. I don't even believe it's in Jane's best interest to have met me, but I did, and now I have to do something about it. About her, about Emily, about our tangled lives. "I felt responsible. But I didn't feel anything else."

"I wouldn't blame you if you did."

I shift myself over her, and Jane spreads her legs to make room for me. I'm not good for her. Not good enough to bend my head and kiss her collarbone. Not good enough to lick away the imprint of my lips. Not good at all. But I can't stop myself. I've tried. I've tried not to feel this way, I've tried not to want her, and it doesn't work. "You think I still want her? Is that it? You think I went there today with the past on my mind?"

I'm kissing up the side of her neck and so I can't see Jane's face when she answers. "Maybe," she breathes. "Maybe."

"I could only think about you. Damn it, Jane. I wanted to walk out of that shitty house as soon as I walked in the door."

I wanted to come back here and be with her, and that's the part I can't say. It's like choking on a mouthful of seawater. I wanted to come back to this place with the certainty of Jane tucked in my pocket. I can't ever send her away again. But if she wants to leave, if she wants her own life away from the wreckage of mine, how could I keep her prisoner here? I couldn't. There's a real possibility she could drown in the weight of all these secrets and all this pain. Who would want to stay for this? For this negotiation with Emily about Paige, and for me, the man who couldn't protect any of them from anything?

"You did," she says softly. "You did come back here."

"Not soon enough."

She doesn't ask me what I was late for, and I don't know. All I know is that every moment away from Jane Mendoza is a knife through the ribs. I'll bleed out from loving her, and I'll deserve it.

Jane puts a hand on the back of my neck and holds tight. "What are we going to do?" she asks.

What the hell are we going to do? I know it's the right thing for Paige to go back with her mother. I know it. Emily was reasonable today. She's done plenty of unreasonable things in the name of staying alive. I'm doing an unreasonable thing right now. But if Paige goes back to her, it will tear a hole in my life. It hurts to imagine it. The little flashes of the life I'd have. No Paige doing her homework at the kitchen table. No

Paige running on the beach. No Jane, beaming at her paintings, at the rocks she likes to collect, at her ruthlessness at Monopoly. Who will Jane have to smile at if Paige isn't here?

No one smiles at me forever. Eventually, I fuck it up beyond repair. I cause too much pain. How long would it take to do the same to Jane? I've already done damage. I can feel it in her body against mine. She's guarded in a way she wasn't before.

"We'll figure it out in the morning." There's nothing to be done about any of this tonight. The problems Emily is facing—that we're all facing—can only be solved in the light of day, with the help of other people, if they're willing to give it. Only one problem can be solved tonight.

Damn me. I want her. More of her. Always more of her. Jane doesn't stop me. She parts her thighs for me and pulls me close. The ocean beats at the shore. Jane doesn't say anything. I don't know if she believes me. She's afraid I'll send her away.

She should be afraid I'll keep her here.

CHAPTER TWELVE

Beau Rochester

THE DISTRICT ATTORNEY'S office shares space with the county courthouse off the town square. I'm at the building, with its red brick and its bell tower, before the janitor finishes unlocking the front door. I drove out to the A-frame as soon as the sun was up and found Emily already awake. Don't know how she couldn't be. The uninsulated A-frame lets in all the sound from the surrounding forest and the birds make a racket. This time, I didn't go in. We talked on the threshold, Emily's voice still rough from sleep or a lack of it.

Nobody will be able to rest until this is solved.

I follow the engraved brass signs and stand beside one of the chairs by the DA's office. The click of high heels on the tile arrives a moment later.

Lauren Michaels comes into view.

She's all grown up now in a skirt suit and jacket. The memories I have of Lauren from high school mainly involve her cheerleading uniform. I was a shallow high school boy. Now I'm a man with a family to protect. She holds a stack of folders tucked into one arm and a travel coffee mug in the other. I step forward as she approaches. My knee protests this. Turns out falling down a cliff tends to linger.

"Rochester," she says. "You're here early."

"You need help with that?" She's balancing her coffee mug on top of the folders and reaching into her purse.

"No," she says, and from her tone I know she's used to this kind of refusal. I catch her sidelong glance at me as she turns the key in the lock. "Thank you," Lauren adds, and then we're stepping inside as she flips on the lights. Lauren's office is off to one side. "Have a seat," she says as she distributes her things neatly on the surface of the desk. "We can get started, if you'd like."

"Thanks for meeting with me."

She arches an eyebrow, takes her seat, and reaches for her coffee. "I got your message on the way in. It sounded urgent."

"Yes." It is urgent. It's all of our lives on the

line. Not the act of living itself, but the shape and form. I want to know whether mine looks like an overfished bay or whether the water teems with silver flashes. All my money and influence will be a cold comfort if I'm left with nothing. I don't deserve much more than that, but for a very limited amount of time, I still have it. "The topic is...delicate."

Lauren checks to make sure the door is closed. It is. "If you're here about the Coach House investigation, I don't have much insight into—"

"It's not about that. It's about Emily Rochester."

An emotion I can't name flashes through her eyes. Lauren's next sip of coffee is studiously deliberate, though her cheeks have gone pink. "I was sorry to hear about her passing."

"It turns out her death was misreported. She's still alive, and back in town."

The travel mug meets the desk with a thunk. "You're kidding."

"I'm not." I can tell Lauren doesn't quite believe me. There's not much trust in her green eyes. She doesn't owe me any. Lauren Michaels wanted to date when we were in school, and she got up the courage to tell me about it. And I, in classic Beau Rochester fashion, blew her off completely. Emily had moved to town by then and all I wanted in the world was to be near her. To impress her. To show her that I was going somewhere. "She's resurfaced in town, and I've had a couple of conversations with her about the night her husband died."

"Her husband. Your brother."

"Yes. The night Rhys died." I don't know how far I can push this. The DA's office is naturally tight with the police force. If Joe's gotten to Lauren before me, she might make the situation worse. But there's no one else to go to. "She's told me that Joe Causey had some involvement with Rhys's death."

This is Lauren's chance to deny it outright. She can express shock at the idea that Joe would ever be involved with something like that. But she just picks up her coffee again. Sips it. Looks at me over the rim of the travel mug. "Seems like everybody's brother played a role."

"He didn't just play a role. If what Emily says is true, he shot Rhys and tried to do the same to her. She's been in hiding ever since."

"And her daughter has been with you." This is known in town. There's no such thing as privacy in a place this size. Everyone came to Rhys's funeral and everyone knew Paige would be coming to live with me. We were the main source of gossip for weeks. "Is she looking to regain custody?"

"Ultimately, yes. But she can't do that unless there's some guarantee of her safety."

"You said you've had a couple of conversations with her?"

"Yes. This morning, and yesterday."

"How did she seem?"

Sad. That's how she seemed. Sad, and tired, and slightly desperate. Like she'd been kept from her own heart. "She was nervous, but determined. Emily wants to get her daughter back."

Lauren presses her lips together. "She's been staying elsewhere, or here in town?"

"Here in town for most of it." In a bare-bones cabin with no furniture and no heat in the winter. If that's not commitment from a woman like Emily Rochester, I don't know what is.

"And she never came forward to claim Paige? Never let on that she was alive?"

"Not until after the fire. Scared Joe as much as it scared me. At the time, I thought it was because he'd grieved for her."

"You have a different opinion now."

The summer day is coming alive outside Lauren's windows. Jane and Paige will be finishing breakfast soon. Making plans to go to the beach or play Monopoly. "Emily Rochester is a lot of things, but she's not a liar."

A slight frown. "I hate to be insensitive, Beau."

"Be insensitive. I'm the one who showed up here uninvited."

She shrugs. "It's a public building. I didn't have any early meetings. Have you considered that your judgment might be clouded by your past history with Emily?"

"I'm not still in love with her, if that's what you're asking."

"I wasn't. No. But this sense that she's being truthful—"

"She's never lied before." I didn't want to get into all this. Still don't. "You know we were dating. You know she ended up with Rhys."

The color in Lauren's cheeks deepens. "I heard things around town. Can't say I was paying much attention at that point."

"Well, if you're going to lie about anything, I'd think you'd start with that. The two of them got together when I was in California. She wasn't the one who broke the news, but she never cowered from it. I think she's telling the truth about Joe Causey. I've seen the way he acts."

"Why are you here instead of her?" Lauren was like this in school. She always wanted to dig into things. I can appreciate it now. Back then, I didn't have eyes for anyone but Emily. It's not lost on me that I could have married a girl like Lauren. It would have been impossible to hide anything from her, though. She'd have seen straight through all the walls I'd put up.

"She obviously has some reservations about Joe knowing she's in town. Too much of a risk." Lauren makes a sound that could be agreement. "Emily asked me to come here and talk to you on the assumption I'd have some sway."

Lauren cracks a smile. "Based on a long-dead high school crush?"

"I guess so."

Good for her. Lauren might not have escaped the way everybody wanted to in high school, but she's come back to a position of power.

The ease of the moment wanes. Lauren's expression sobers. My heart pushes at the boundaries of my rib cage. She's either about to tell me to get the fuck out of here and not bother her again, or she's going to tell me something I can use. "I need to be able to count on your discretion."

"You can." I'm not in the habit of running my

mouth to anyone in town. My time is taken up with Paige, and with Jane, and there's nobody else I want to talk to right now, other than Mateo. I'm not going to say all this to Lauren. If she doesn't know by now that I practically became a recluse at Coach House, then nothing I can say will convince her.

"You're not the first person to bring Joe Causey to our attention." Interesting. *Our attention* means the DA's office, not just the prosecuting attorney. "There may be an ongoing investigation into his conduct. If there were an investigation like that, it would have to proceed with extreme caution."

She's watching me with extreme caution now. "That's good."

"You might be able to help."

"Anything I could do." My throat has gone tight with the promise. Making sure Joe's out of the picture clears the way for everything else. It clears the way for Emily to get Paige back, and for Jane to leave me and go on to a life that's worthy of her. I'd be adrift again and sinking fast. It would be right. I've been a coward and a bastard. That's what would be worthy of me.

"Evidence," says Lauren. "Evidence pertaining to the subject is always very helpful. This could include things like a written statement or other documents that would shine light on—"

"Like a diary?"

She inclines her head. "In some cases, first-person accounts have been useful for constructing a narrative." That's all it ever is, isn't it? Constructing a narrative. We tell the stories we want to believe about other people. In some cases, they turn out to be true. "As far as current statements, anything we received right now would have to be vetted, but it's always better to have these things in hand rather than go searching for them at a later date."

"Where would a person drop those kinds of documents off?"

"Directly to me. And I don't mean an envelope addressed to me, care of the DA's office. I mean directly into my hands."

"Understood." I stand up again and reach across the desk to shake Lauren's hand. "Thanks for the talk."

"Today," she says, rising too. "That's an ideal timeline. And then sit tight."

CHAPTER THIRTEEN

Jane Mendoza

PAIGE BUILDS SANDCASTLES with the sea breeze in her hair. Her focus is intent on the towers she shapes with small hands. One springs up, then another. She creates a ridge between the two of them and curls her fingers over the top to make a wall. I woke up to her standing at the side of the bed this morning, eyes wide. "It's time to get up," she whispered. "Beau's not here."

He left a note on the bedside table.

Going into town to meet with the prosecutor. Back before lunch.

So we ate breakfast. I drowned Paige's pancakes in syrup until she dissolved into laughter, and then I packed a towel and a plastic bucket and shovel into a bag and went to the shore. We put on sunscreen.

I had a vague idea of what it would be like to

get out of my old life. College. Loans, somehow. Working and attending class and eventually getting a job as a social worker. I never pictured sitting on a beach in Maine watching a little girl make sandcastles.

I never pictured waiting for my former boss to come back to this strange, unfinished place we've found ourselves in. It seems more important than ever to figure things out.

That process, and its end, is going to be painful.

Paige glances up at me from her sandcastle and raises her eyebrows.

"It's cool," I tell her. "Are you going to build all four walls?"

"Towers first," she says decisively. One more glance at me, and then she's looking past me, over my shoulder. I'm hoping it's Beau. I want to know what piece of information he's carved out of his meeting with the prosecutor and I want to know if there's any hint of where we should go next. Either way, someone gets hurt. If he keeps Paige, Emily will be devastated. And if Paige goes with her…

I don't want to think about it anymore. I know what it looks like when children are taken from their parents. Or, if they don't have parents, the people who have stood in their place. It's a terrible scene even when everyone agrees that it's for the best. Knowing it's right doesn't soften the blow.

A shadow blocks out the sun from one direction. I take a deep breath and face it. Face whatever he's going to say.

Only it's not Beau.

"Noah. Oh my God. What are you doing here?" I scramble up from the towel and throw my arms around him. His body is stiff, his expression haggard and irritated. His clothes are rumpled like he came straight from work and got on a plane. A ratty backpack is slung over one of his shoulders. "Are you okay?"

He looks from me to Paige and back again. I see the beach, and the inn, from his eyes. This is the kind of place we never would have dreamed of in the foster home. This is the kind of place rich people stay when they want a break from their easy lives.

"Who are you?" asks Paige. She doesn't look thrilled to see Noah. Compared to Beau Rochester, he looks rough. Too thin and without any of the markers a visitor to the beach would normally have. He's not wearing a swimsuit or upscale dock shoes. He's in jeans with worn knees and a t-shirt that looks like it might come apart at the seams.

"This is my friend," I tell her. "Go ahead and keep building your castle."

I tug Noah a few steps away, and Paige, thankfully, goes back to her work without a fuss.

"What is happening to you?" He looks worse than tired. The ever-present circles under his eyes are darker than I've ever seen them. "What the hell, Jane? You came back to town and then you disappeared. You didn't answer my calls. I thought something happened to you."

"I'm sorry." That's my fault. I haven't paid a second of attention to my phone since I walked into my apartment in Houston and found Emily there. "I'm really sorry, Noah. I should have let you know what was happening."

He makes a go-ahead gesture, his eyes boring into mine.

"I can't say much here." I tip my head toward Paige, hoping he'll understand. "But when I got back to Houston, someone was waiting for me."

"Someone who ran you out of town?"

"Someone from here. Her mom," I say in a low voice, though the sea breeze and the waves should be enough to cover the sound. "Emily. She asked me to come back here with her."

Noah's face is twisted in disgust. "So, what?

You just hopped on a plane with her and came back without a word to anyone? How could you think that was okay?"

Guilt heats my face. "I know it's not okay. I didn't have much of a choice at the time."

He scoffs. "She paid you to abandon your life, then."

"No. She didn't pay me. Nobody is paying me. I'm here because I want to be here."

Noah looks like he doesn't recognize me. Like the two of us didn't spend years relying on each other to get through the hell we were living in. "Nobody's paying you, but look at this." He waves toward the inn. The sand. The stretch of beach with expensive houses tucked into the dunes. "This is all bullshit. You were going to college. You were going to make the world a better place. Now you're some socialite wife?"

"What? We're not—no." Shame is a deep sunburn. "I'm not anyone's wife."

"But he's not paying you. You're just here to be with him and his kid."

"Yes," I say, before I can stop myself. "Yes. I'm here to be with him. I don't know what it all means yet. I had unfinished business here. I'm allowed to finish it."

He runs a hand through his hair, appalled.

"You're with him, then. You fell for him so hard that even after he kicked you to the curb, you're still willing to crawl back and work for him for free."

The way he says *work for him* makes it sound filthy. Like I'm a mistress or a prostitute. I don't have any good arguments against either of those things. What people do is their business, as long as it doesn't hurt anyone else, but Noah's words are meant to make me feel like shit.

"If you're trying to convince me to come back to Houston, this isn't the way to do it." I check on Paige. She's on the third tower of her sandcastle now. A big enough wave could pull it under, but I'm not going to make her start over. I'll help her rebuild the damn thing if that's what happens. "You want to come here and tell me that I should be doing something different? I'm allowed to make my own choices."

"I'm not trying to convince you of anything. You could have said something to me. You could have told me, *Noah, I'm running back to Beau Rochester because I couldn't handle one night back in my old life. I'm too good for it now.*"

"Are you sure you want to be saying this?" I don't let the tears stinging my eyes fall. "Be really sure. Because you can't shove the words back into your mouth once they're out. You can't take them back."

He pinches his lips shut. He's tired. I can see that. Exhausted, even. Life has not been kind to Noah, and it wasn't kind to me, and for a long time the only kindness we found was in each other. Maybe if he weren't being such an asshole, I could muster up more empathy for him. But he came here to leave his anger at my feet, and I can't carry it right now. My hands are full.

"Are you okay?" This is the question he should have led with. He might have if things weren't so hard. But things are what they are. I'm not going to be a pushover with Beau, and I'm not going to slip into my old role with Noah. "I'm worried sick about you. I came here because I can't understand what's happening to you. You used to be open with me about stuff like that. You came back—" He shakes his head. Looks away. "You came back with your eyes all red like it was the end of the world. And then I find out you're right back here."

"How?" I didn't tell anyone where I was going. "How would you know where I was?"

He sighs. "When you weren't at home the next day, I called every place I could think of. You haven't been anywhere but this inn and the airport. The lady at the front desk told me you were here."

"I'm here, and I'm fine." I press the back of my hand to my eyes. No tears. Not now. After everything that's happened, the last thing Paige needs is to see me break down because of a confrontation on the beach.

"Are you staying?" Noah asks.

I don't know the answer to that question. It depends on the answers to a hundred other questions. All of them are wrapped up in each other. Paige and Emily are a complicated tangle and at the center of it all is Beau Rochester. I might tell myself that I came back here for Emily, but I also came for myself.

"I don't think it's a good time to talk about this."

Noah's chin comes up. "Then we'll talk later."

"You can text me—"

"No. We'll talk later. I'm not getting on a plane today. I've got a motel off the highway." He takes one last look at the inn and the beach and the blue water rolling in over itself. "The Jane I knew would have split the room with me. Looks like you've moved up in the world."

All the biting things I could say in response to this wither and die. I don't want them in the air between us, or in our memories. "You should go."

"Yeah." Noah shrugs, like it was nothing for him to walk down to this beach in this place. "I'll talk to you soon."

"Let me know when you get back to the motel," I say automatically. This is what we've always done for each other. We check in, and make sure the other person's still breathing. We remind each other to deadbolt the door. The difference now is that I don't want to be protected from my life. I want it to belong to me.

"I will," answers Noah. He's turned away already. I don't think he's telling the truth. I don't think he'll text me when he arrives.

I don't have it in me to watch him until he disappears behind the inn. I don't want to know if he looks back, or if he doesn't. My throat feels tight with tears. Sand has collected in the towel, so I gauge the wind and shake it out so it doesn't get in Paige's eyes, then sit back down on the edge. She's crouched down behind her castle, her hands smoothing down the sand. With a brisk brush of her palms, she stands up and puts her hands on her hips.

"You look sad," she says. "Do you not like that guy?"

"No. I like him a lot."

She narrows her eyes. "You don't look at him the way you look at Beau."

"How do I look at Beau?"

Paige makes her eyes wide and moony and tilts her head. "Like this."

It makes me laugh in spite of myself. It's true that I don't look at Noah like that. I've looked at him lots of different ways. As my co-conspirator and friend. Sometimes as my protector. But I've never felt the way I feel when I look at Beau.

Noah's right. I'm different now, but not in the way he says. I haven't sold out or given in. I'm making my own way.

CHAPTER FOURTEEN

Beau Rochester

PAIGE DIPS A fish stick into ketchup and peers across the table at me. In the scheme of things, not much happened today. I met with the prosecutor. I took a statement from Emily and had it printed at the public library. I came home and was generally useless while Jane worked on schoolwork with Paige. I tried to help with a few of the problems, but Paige didn't want my input. Jane's is better.

Nothing much happened, but I'm as worn as if I'd spent all day on a fishing boat. If I didn't know better, I'd think I had a sunburn. My skin is on fire with Jane's proximity and how tenuous everything is. She came back to my bed, and back to my arms.

It would be simple for her with another man. She wouldn't be wary of him sending her away.

He wouldn't be foolish enough to do it in the first place.

The situation with Emily hangs over the table. I told Jane last night we'd figure it out in the morning, and then I left her sleeping. The truth is that I don't want to talk about it. I don't want to talk about Emily. I don't want to watch Jane's eyes darken when she remembers how I sent her away. I want to take her to bed and make her forget.

Jane meets my eyes and smiles.

It tugs at some soft, hidden part of me. After everything that's happened, there's still innocence in her smile. A sense of hope. It's always been there. Drew me to her the very first night we met.

I don't know any way to figure this out that doesn't end up hurting her. Or me. Or both of us. That's why part of me wishes I didn't need her so much. She doesn't deserve to weather this with me.

"My sandcastle had four towers." Paige has the air of a person who feels a little sorry for anyone with a lower-quality sandcastle. "Next time, I'm doing eight."

"Are you going to put hotels in all of them?" It's a Monopoly reference.

She takes a bite of her fish stick and narrows

her eyes at me while she chews it. A sign that she's thinking about what I said and probably finding several flaws with it. "There wouldn't be enough room for hotels in those towers."

"Imaginary hotels, maybe."

Paige adds another pool of ketchup to her plate. "The guy at the beach didn't notice the towers. He was too busy being mad at Jane."

My blood freezes. Jane's hands tighten around her mug. "Mad at Jane for what?"

"I thought we could talk about it after dinner." Jane's voice is soft, but it's steady. Her tone holds a warning. We're not going to discuss it now.

"For not visiting." Paige tips her head back and drops the last bite of fish stick into her mouth. "I'm going to finish my drawing."

"Five minutes," Jane calls after her. "Then it's bath time."

"Who the hell was mad at you at the beach?"

"Noah came to see me." She stands up and gathers up her plate and Paige's. I take mine to the sink and Jane comes to stand off my left elbow. "I can't put the dishes in the dishwasher unless you move, Beau."

"I'll do it. You tell me what happened."

"When Paige is asleep."

It pisses me off, how stoic and unrelenting she's being about this. My mind swings between imagining the worst—a shouting match in front of Paige, maybe even threats of violence—and trusting that Jane would have told me if that had happened. I can't decide between the two. So much remains unresolved between us that I couldn't blame her if she wanted to handle it by herself. I could only blame me. For sending her away and breaking her trust. For letting my guard down enough to leave her here with Paige, alone on the beach. By the time Paige nods off to the sound of Jane's voice reading The Giving Tree, I'm all out of patience.

Jane slides her arm gently out from under Paige's head. I help her climb out of the bed. We bump into each other, both of us reaching to pull up the covers. Jane concedes without a word, then goes to her room.

I follow her. I make damn sure to shut the door as quietly as I can. I don't want any chance of Paige waking up.

"Did he hurt you?" If he did, I'll kill him.

"Jesus, Beau. He didn't touch me. Noah wouldn't do that." Jane lays the book down on her own bedside table. She forgot to leave it in Paige's room. She lets out a sigh and runs both hands over her hair. The motion makes her arch her back and I'm nearly eaten up with desire and a base need to protect her. "He got worried about me when he found out I left town. He wanted to make sure I was okay."

"By fighting with you in front of a child?"

"It wasn't fighting. Not exactly." Jane crosses her arms over her chest. "He was upset I hadn't told him I was leaving, and I didn't tell him I was here. All it would have taken was one phone call."

Jealousy squeezes at my stomach. "You don't answer to him."

"He's my friend. My oldest, best friend."

"How did this fight go?" I want to touch her. Hold her. But I can't do it yet, because once I get my hands on her, there won't be any more discussion. "Why does Paige know so much about it?"

"He didn't shout. He was angry. He was...surprised. That I'd be in a place like this, with a man like you. He felt like I'd abandoned my entire life in Houston and given up on everything I wanted to do. We'd never have known this kind of place existed when we were younger. He feels like I turned my back on him and I'm getting used by all the rich people here."

"I want to punch him." I want this asshole

from Texas to understand that he can't just come here and disrupt everyone's lives. He can't scare Paige. He can't intimidate Paige. "If he comes back here, you'll tell me."

"No." Jane chews at the inside of her cheek. "He's right."

"What?" Ridiculous. Noah isn't right about anything.

"What am I doing?" A disbelieving smile flickers across her face. "I had dreams, and they're getting derailed. By sex with you."

"Let's have sex, then. If I'm going to derail you like that, I want it to be happening already."

"No, this is what I'm saying." A pleading frustration comes to Jane's eyes. "What about college?"

"You can go to college."

She gives me a look. "And what? You'll pay for it?"

"Yes."

Jane rolls her eyes at me. "Like a sugar daddy?"

"No. Not like that." The thought of that kind of arrangement with Jane feels slimy and disgusting. I don't want to pay her for her time. I don't want to buy her affection. I want to give her everything so I can watch her dreams come true.

Every last one of them.

"How exactly would it be different?" Jane asks this question like she already knows the answer. "You'd pay the bill and come and fuck me in my dorm room?"

"Jesus. No."

"You wouldn't fuck me in my dorm room? There are always strings attached when it comes to money, Beau. Even you can't deny it."

"You think I'd pay for college to force you into having sex with me?"

"You don't have to force me."

"Exactly." Anger bursts out of me. "I want you to be able to go to college and not worry about a damn thing, Jane. Why do you think it would become some filthy arrangement?"

"Why wouldn't it?" Real fear widens her eyes, but it's gone almost instantly. "We weren't supposed to get involved in the first place, but we did. Now that I'm not the nanny, I don't know how this plays out. Do you only want me if you're forbidden to have me?"

A direct hit. "Maybe I do," I shoot back, regretting it as soon as the words are out of my mouth. "Do you only want me because I'm a blank check?"

Her mouth drops open. "I've never wanted

you for your money."

"Bullshit."

"I wanted the job for money." Jane's eyes flash. "I wanted you because you were convenient. And I thought you might pay me extra."

"Little liar," I say, my voice soft. "You wish that was the only reason you slept with me."

"I'd rather sleep alone tonight." Jane lifts her chin and dares me to argue with her. I want to do it. I want to invade her space and pin her to the bed and kiss every stupid thing I've said to her tonight off her skin. I'd do it if I thought she'd let me.

Jane only pauses to let Kitten dart into her room, and then she shuts the door tight. It's like being locked out in the rain. My own room at the inn feels cold and empty without her, but I'm sure as hell not going to go beg for her to let me in. If Jane wants to be alone tonight, then fine. Let her sleep alone.

That attitude lasts for about five seconds. Hope crushes it under its heel. I hope to hear her footsteps in the hall while I brush my teeth. I hope again while I plug in the charger to my phone and check for any new emails from the prosecutor. I hope I'll hear her as I turn out the light and lie there in a bed that's devoid of any real pleasure, because she's not in it.

There's only so much scrolling I can do before my eyes are burning and my head is heavy. At the same time, I'm so wired I don't know how I'll fall asleep. It's too early, but it feels too late. It feels impossible if she's not here. Forget the phone. Forget everything.

I can feel Jane nearby. I hate that she's so close, and I can't see her. But part of me is glad that she's here at all. Pissed at me or not. Speaking to me or not. That feeling will wear through by morning. Maybe my resolve will, too. Maybe I'll get out of this goddamn bed and go knock on her door until she agrees to talk to me.

I could do it.

I could.

The inn settles around me. The building's not new construction. Floors creak as the wind shifts the structure around us by minuscule degrees. The sound of ocean waves rushes at the windows. An owl calls.

No footsteps. Has she fallen asleep already? I know how long the days are with Paige. You love her to death, and all that love is exhausting. You try to be the best version of yourself because she's just a kid and half the time you fail. Jane never does, though. She leans into caring for Paige like she's done it all her life. Jane is a million times better at being a parent for Paige than I am. She's a better person. If anything, she deserves a night away from me.

I keep turning the argument over in my head. Anger comes back like a rain shower. On and off. On and off. I don't want her to think those things about me, much less say them to my face.

What she said could be true. I could always be looking for something that's not available to me. Safer that way. For me, but also for the people I want to be with. Love is a blood sport.

I keep hoping anyway. The night drags me under bit by bit while I listen for the soft sound of her footsteps. When I finally fall asleep, I dream of that sound.

Jane herself never appears.

CHAPTER FIFTEEN

Emily Rochester

MY EYES ACHE from crying. I didn't expect to get emotional in the prosecutor's office. The questioning got intense. They were trying to trip me up, asking the same question backwards and forwards. Shouting when I didn't answer fast enough. But I understand. It's not something to be taken lightly, a man's career. A man's life. My brother. *Why did you do this, Joe?*

Fireflies dance among the trees, the only light in the forest. The moon can't reach this deep into the trees. I'm alone. The A-frame has been a sanctuary for me—as well as a prison. I sit on the front steps, which is as far as I venture most days.

Sometimes the solitude has felt like punishment.

A crack of a branch. I freeze, like a deer. It could be anything in the woods. A possum. A bear. As long as it's an animal, I'm fine. The true danger comes in the form of humans.

Sometimes hunters roam these woods, though it's not hunting season. Poachers, then. I won't judge them. I know what it's like to go hungry. I'd rather their children eat. Still, I have to worry about discovery. It wouldn't do for Joe to catch wind of a woman living out in the woods.

We can barely hear anything this far from the city. Only the occasional dirge from the distant ferry.

Another crack. I go completely still.

I've become used to the ambient sounds of nature. The coo of a bird. The patter of squirrels. Even the chaos has a sort of pattern, and this doesn't fit into it.

An intruder.

I consider running into the cabin, but whoever it is sounds close. I would make more noise crossing the old, creaky porch than I would staying still. I can't bring myself to sit, though. I did too much of that before Rhys died—sitting. Waiting. Hoping that if I stayed quiet enough, I could earn some peace. I learned to face my fears in the freezing cold water.

I fought to survive—and I've never stopped fighting since.

Now I reach for the pistol that I've been carrying for months.

My bare feet are silent on the cool dirt. I press my body against the slanting edge of the cabin and peer around the corner. A shadow shifts. Faint moonlight glints off something metal—a zipper, maybe. Closer. My heart rate spikes. They're coming closer. Cold sweat washes over me, along with a grim sense of certainty. There are a hundred specific fears, ghosts from my past, being discovered, that I didn't have time to worry about the more general threat every woman faces—being alone in the dark with a strange man.

Boots land solid on the packed earth.

Before he can round the corner, I step out and aim. "Who are you?"

The shadow pauses. It blends back into the night. Only his voice marks him as more than a figment of my imagination. "Christ. You're going to hurt someone with that thing."

"That's kind of the point," I say, dropping the muzzle to point down. He's an asshole, sure. But I'm not going to shoot him. Not now, anyway. "What are you doing here?"

Mateo steps closer, his features just as handsome veiled in night. "Thought you might be plotting some shit, and it's my job to make sure you don't fuck Beau over."

Indignation makes me snort. "You caught me. I'm planning a coup with the trees."

One dark eyebrow rises. "I wouldn't put it past you."

"It's creepy, you coming around here at night. Like you're a ghost."

He snorts. "You would know something like haunting people."

Yes, I did hang around the Coach House. And then the inn. It hurt me to be away from Paige, to wonder whether she's okay. "What are you really doing here?"

"The truth?"

"Please."

"The truth is I was checking on you. It's not safe for a woman to live alone in these woods. Anything can happen."

"Nowhere is safe for me." Not with Joe looking for me. And especially now that he probably found the plane records. It means he'll know for sure I'm back in Eben Cape. He's surely been hoping that I ran away to some tropical island. Or maybe that I died in the water.

"No," Mateo agrees, his voice soft. "That beautiful old Coach House wasn't safe for you, was it? And no one noticed. No one cared."

My lips twist. I was the stereotypical battered woman. Afraid to run away. Afraid to be at home. I'm so freaking tired of being afraid. "So you believe me now?"

"I've always believed Rhys was a bastard."

I roll my eyes. "So it's less about believing me and more about knowing him."

"I have sisters. I wouldn't want them to be with a bastard like him."

That makes me turn away. "I wish people could care about other people. Without needing to have a sister or a daughter. I wish people could *believe* people. No one should be slapped because they made a shitty chicken cacciatore."

"Is that why Rhys hit you?"

Humiliation heats my cheeks. "Why am I talking about this with you?"

"Because you need someone to talk to, and I'm the only one here right now."

"There's the trees," I say. "They've heard a lot of my secrets."

"And they believe you?"

"They know what it's like to be chopped down and broken into pieces and shredded until they're nothing. They know what it's like to endure without having a voice."

He steps close, but I don't turn around. My eyes close against the black night. I don't want to see him. Or hear him. Or *want* him.

His heat is strangely seductive. He's a ridiculously handsome man, but that's not why I want him. Especially not when it's pitch black. I can't even see him, but he still calls to something inside me. I shouldn't want any man. They're all dangerous. All a risk I've learned not to take. This one's worse than most. He mocks me during my most painful moments. And he didn't believe me at the cabin. "I do believe you," he murmurs, as if he can hear my thoughts.

Words catch in my throat. I don't know whether it's his trust I want, his acceptance, his comfort. Or whether I need those things, and he's the only one here.

Then his heat fades away. Footsteps crunch through the woods.

I'm alone again.

CHAPTER SIXTEEN

Jane Mendoza

THE MEETING ROOM smells like coffee and donut glaze and sharp carpet cleaner. Beau sits next to me at a big wooden table across from the local prosecutor, whose name is Lauren Michaels. She wears a sharp gray skirt suit.

Beau's in a suit, too.

That had been a surprise, when he came down the stairs of the inn. Even Kitten was curious about his polished shoes. I'm used to seeing him in cable-knit sweaters and thick jeans. He was sexy in those, but he's breathtaking in a suit. I can picture him in a high-powered business meeting in California, shaking hands over a deal that would change his life. Well, I suppose this deal can change lives, too.

I put a sweater on with yoga pants, since I don't have any business casual. Even if I did, it wouldn't look like hers. Lauren looks comfortable in it. Beau looks more than comfortable in his.

I've never been more uncomfortable in my life.

Except for when Emily was pointing her gun at me. That felt pretty terrible.

Beau and I are not speaking. It was a tense, silent car ride, with him in his fancy clothes and me in my yoga pants. He looks like he's a million miles above me in his outfit. He looks rich, and I look like I could desperately use a sugar daddy.

Emily would look right next to him. I don't.

And I don't know what to say about last night. Beau's too busy stewing about it to say anything. I can feel his frustration simmering. If he wants to argue with me, he should just do it. We'll be miserable until this is resolved.

I'll be miserable.

"Any minute now." Lauren checks her watch. "How are you holding up?"

"Fine," answers Beau. "Be better for everyone if this was resolved. Paige, especially."

"How's she doing? Is she with your friend?"

"With Mateo, and she's good."

Mateo promised Paige to build the world's biggest sandcastle this morning. A competitive gleam lit her eyes. I would give just about anything to be building a sandcastle right now.

"You remember my sister, Carrie? She just had her baby."

They chat about the baby and I try my best to follow along. Of course Beau remembers her sister. Wow, he can't believe she's already had three children.

Wasn't she a year behind us in school? Oh, two.

"Sorry we're late." A man steps through the door carrying a Styrofoam cup. He's followed by two other people, one man and one woman. He drops a file folder onto the table and sticks out his hand to both of us. "Shane Williams. Internal affairs. This is Paul and Susan. They'll be at the meeting tomorrow. We'll need you there, Mr. Rochester."

"Just me?"

"Yes."

The three of them take their seats. Lauren gestures to Shane. "Why don't we go straight to your questions for Beau and Jane?"

Beau and Jane. The way she says our names makes it sound like they belong together. I'm not sure they do, in the end. Judging from last night's conversation, Beau and I have very different ideas about how our lives will look.

"As you know, we're here to discuss Detective

Joe Causey. Because it's an ongoing investigation, we can't comment on the details."

"Move on to the questions." Beau's being exactly as surly as he was the first night I came to Coach House. This time he isn't up against a stubborn little girl and a kitten. He's up against the entirety of the law enforcement system.

"When was the last time you saw Emily Rochester? Before the events of this week?" Shane takes out a legal pad and a pen.

"About eight years ago."

"And when did you become aware that she was still alive?"

"A week ago. Joe Causey came to the inn where we were staying with video footage of her from one of the stores downtown."

"What was his demeanor like during that encounter?"

Beau frowns. "It surprised him. He was shaken up. Didn't know what to do about it."

"Ms. Mendoza—" Shane glances over his legal pad. "You met with Detective Joe Causey on a couple of occasions, right?"

"He came to my hospital room and accused me of starting the fire at Coach House."

The prosecutor exchanges a look with one of the people on the internal affairs team. Shane takes notes. "And he interviewed you at the inn as part of his investigation."

"That conversation was bullshit. He was more concerned with details of my will than the fire." Beau folds his arms over his chest, glowering.

He'd changed his will to include me in it.

Joe was the one to give me that information. If Beau had died in the fire, I would be rich beyond my wildest dreams. It makes my throat tight with frustration. I'd never choose money over Beau Rochester. I've spent my life thinking that money would solve all my problems if I could get enough of it. Not a billion dollars. Enough to afford food and a place to live and a second to breathe.

"Your will?"

"I added Jane as a beneficiary."

"Without telling me," I say, fear turning to frustration.

"You didn't need to know."

"So Causey's thinking was that the change in the will made Jane a suspect," Shane says.

"The changes were made without her knowledge," adds Lauren. "He didn't follow that line of investigation any further after the last meeting."

"I never asked for your money," I mutter

back.

"In a way you did, because you took my job offer in the first place."

"And the internal investigation won't focus on that," answers Shane.

"No," says Lauren. "Our sole focus is on the Emily Rochester case."

"It's not just a job anymore. It's your life. And obviously I'm never going to fit into it if you think you have to give me with money." My heart pounds. This is my real, true fear. That women like Emily Rochester are the only ones who will ever have a place in Beau's life. That they're the only ones who can have a non-transactional relationship with him.

"That's bullshit," mutters Beau.

Lauren raises her eyebrows. "Do we need to take a break?"

"No," we both answer at the same time.

"What we've found in our investigation is that Joe did more than siphon drug money. He took bribes to make evidence disappear. We need to know what cases were impacted."

I can't keep my mouth shut. "It's not bullshit."

Shane's answering Lauren now, but I'm not listening.

"It *is* bullshit. So you can be with a broke college student, but not a billionaire? I don't know how one plane ride with Emily made you think I'm trying to buy you like a whore."

"That's what it means when you pay for college in exchange for being together."

"I'm not fucking paying for college in exchange for being together, Jane."

Lauren drums her red-tipped fingers on the table. "Can we stay on topic? The diary presented some necessary background for the criminal case. Causey wasn't just stealing evidence. Her account details quite a history of domestic violence from her husband. I think Joe wanted it as blackmail against Rhys. I think he was using her to manipulate him."

"I'm scared that's what it means," I whisper. "You have to admit—"

Beau slams his palm down on the tabletop and turns to face me, his eyes burning into mine. "If you want me to be your sugar daddy, fine. If you don't, I'll give away the fucking money. Goddamn it, Jane. Go to college. Don't go to college. Use my money. Don't. I don't care about the money. I just want to be with you."

"Why?" I ask, almost pleading, desperate.

"Because I love you."

A ringing silence descends upon the table.

Because I love you. He just said that in the prosecutor's meeting room.

Everyone is staring at us. I've never heard him sound this angry, but it doesn't matter if he's angry, it doesn't matter. It doesn't even matter if Lauren the prosecutor stands up and says the meeting is over due to terrible behavior on the part of Beau Rochester. She probably wouldn't do that, because she's not a judge, but I don't know, and I don't care.

Tears gather in the corners of my eyes. "You love me?"

"Yes," he snaps, sounding furious.

I'm trembling in the creaky wood and cloth chair. Part of me wants to deny it. The old insecurities surfacing. And then confidence overtakes me. Certainty. *Love.*

I lean toward him.

As soon as my lips brush against his, I feel all the tension in him. It was a long night for us both. Some of it escapes on a sigh. "I don't care about the money," he says again, his voice low and intimate even at this meeting table. "I'll give it all away."

"Keep me." That's all I want. I want to have a place in Beau's life even if I'm not Lauren

Michaels or Emily Rochester. I'll never be those people. Even if I go to college and marry Beau and move back to this town with him, I'll always be Jane Mendoza. Myself.

"I will," he says, and it's a solemn promise. I can hear the *bang bang* of a soda can falling down vending machine somewhere in a nearby break room. We're in the middle of the courthouse. This isn't the place to make those kinds of promises… Or maybe it's exactly the right place. I cling to him, and he drags me close enough that it hurts.

It hurts perfectly.

I lean forward again. First he lets me kiss him. It's a passive thing, which is strange for Beau. He accepts it, maybe to prove something. Whatever the reason, it doesn't last long. His hand curves around the back of my neck. He holds me still as his mouth turns aggressive. Lips press against mine. Tongue invades. He's commanding with every stroke, and I obey. It's explicit, this kiss. We aren't touching anywhere except our mouths and his hand behind my neck, but it feels like sex. It feels like we're having sex in the space of one heartbeat. And two. And three. It feels like we're finding completion in the stroke of his tongue against mine.

Someone clears their throat.

I don't want to let go of him. I'd rather climb into his lap and let him carry me back to the inn. I'm not naive enough to think this one kiss has solved everything, but I feel a sense of hope.

Whatever comes next, we'll face it together.

Someone coughs.

Beau breaks the kiss but presses his forehead against mine. Our breaths mingle. The air in our lungs is the same. The molecules we inhabit are the same.

Our beating hearts are the same.

"Okay," Shane from internal affairs says. Right. The next thing we'll face is all the people who just watched us fight and kiss. "What do you guys think? Are we good to keep going? Or do you guys want to make out a little more?"

CHAPTER SEVENTEEN

Jane Mendoza

NOAH'S STAYING AT the cheapest possible motel in town. Technically, I'm not sure it is in town. It's out on the highway directly across from the "entering Eben Cape" sign. I don't know whether that means it's in town or the nearby township. Either way, it's scary. A gravel driveway skims a beat-up sidewalk. There are eight rooms, plus a small lobby with an apartment above it.

"You sure you want to stop here?" the Uber driver asks me. It's the same man who dropped me off at Coach House.

"I'll be okay."

He hesitates, but eventually drives off.

Looking at this hotel makes me feel twisted inside. This is where I came from. A run-down collection of rooms with scuffs on every door. They've all weathered a fight between someone on the inside and someone on the outside. Without Beau's money, this is all I can afford too. With Beau, I feel like a princess. We used to daydream about lives like mine when we were in the foster home.

"A person just to cook for you," Noah would whisper, late at night.

"More than one bathroom. One of those ones with the towels you're not supposed to touch."

The last door on the left opens. Noah looks out at me. "Are you coming in or are you just going to stand in the parking lot?" I go over to the door. He leans against the frame with his hands in his pockets. "Hey."

"Hi."

"You don't have to come in if you don't want to." His brittle tone suggests I might be too good for this kind of place.

"Stop it." I push past him and go into the room. The covers on one of the beds have been shoved back like he tried to sleep, tossed and turned, and gave up. Noah shuts and locks the door. "I didn't like how things ended on the beach. And you didn't text me to say you got here okay."

"Yeah, well, you didn't text me to say you were leaving Houston. I guess we're even."

"Honestly, Noah, it doesn't feel that great to be even." It feels like shit, actually. I've known him longer than I've known anyone. This isn't how it should go between us. "I didn't come here to fight with you about who texted or who didn't text. I wanted to talk to you."

Noah goes over and flips the covers up on the bed, making it in a sloppy, haphazard way. Then he sits down on the edge and gestures at the other bed. I can feel the springs through the mattress when I sit down and fling my purse onto the bed.

"I know you're pissed."

"I'm not pissed." He runs his hands over his hair, which is a wreck. He has smudges under his eyes. "I'm tired."

"If I could have texted you and given you a warning, I would have. This isn't because I didn't want to tell you."

"Then why didn't you?"

"Because Paige's mom was upset when she came to my apartment. Really upset. She had a gun."

His eyes go wide. "What the hell, Jane? You could have been killed."

"I know that. But she didn't kill me. She wanted help, and I wanted to help her. And what I really want, Noah, is to be here."

"How can you say that when she brought you here at gunpoint?"

"Am I at gunpoint now?"

Noah stares at me, bewildered. "No. That doesn't mean it's a good place for you. It doesn't mean it's a safe place for you."

"It's the right place for me." I take a deep breath and try to see things from his point of view. It hurts. What I'm doing now wasn't in the cards when we made our plans. "That doesn't change the fact that you're my best friend."

"Doesn't it?" I can tell how hard he's trying not to sound angry. "I wanted you to go places, Janie. Do something with your life. Not disappear into the East Coast."

And forget about me. Noah doesn't have to say this part.

"I know it felt like I disappeared, but that's not what's happening. I'm choosing this. I love Beau and Paige, and I belong here. I'm choosing this for me."

"You're sure?" Noah swallows, and now his expression is consumed with sadness. "I want you to be happy. It kept me up nights, worrying about you."

"You don't have to worry about me." I put all my confidence into my voice. "I understand that you will. We'll always worry about each other, and care about each other, but—not like that. This is where I should be."

He stands up and paces to the door, patting his pockets for cigarettes. I grab my purse and follow him. Outside, the air is fresh and clean. The parking lot is empty. It's like the start of a book. Anything could happen, anything at all. Noah lights a cigarette and leans against the door to his motel room. I lean against the siding next to him. We both look out onto the empty parking lot. Cheap as this place is, it's still surrounded by trees.

"I want you to come home with me." Noah doesn't look at me when he says it.

"I know."

Silence falls over the empty parking lot. We're both going to have to call other people for a ride out of here. We won't be leaving in the same car. I can feel the fight going out of him.

"Is it because he has money?" I hear the pain behind the causal question. Noah doesn't have the kind of money Beau has. The kind of money Beau has is a fantasy for people like us. A dream that would never come true. "I wouldn't blame you if it was."

Maybe it would be kinder to lie to him. To

say that it is about the money. Noah might accept it. Money is a way out of a hard life, after all. But I can't start lying to him now, even if the truth hurts.

"I'm in love with him."

Noah blows out a cloud of smoke. His nod is a resigned one. Even if we stay in touch, it's never going to be the same after this. My mind wanders through the life I could have had if Noah and I had gotten together. There would have been no interview with the nanny agency. We would have had a cheap apartment, but we wouldn't spend much time there, because we'd be working. We'd go to dollar movies at the discount theater and constantly be checking our bank accounts, but we'd laugh. And dream. I might not have gone to college, in the end. I might not have fallen in love with him. I might have contented myself with what I had right in front of me.

"You're never coming back, are you?"

No. Not like he means. I'll never move back into my old apartment in Houston with plans to stay. I'm going to follow my dreams, and my dreams are bigger than that place.

"I'm sure I'll visit."

He laughs. "Don't say that, Janie."

"I'll try to visit."

Noah puts out his cigarette on the cracked sidewalk and looks me in the eye. "I hope he's everything you want."

"He is." I can tell he doesn't believe me. I can tell he's hoping I'll change my mind and go back to our old life with him. "You know, I wouldn't have gotten here without you."

That's the thing about making it anywhere you want to go. It takes other people. Without them, you just give up.

Noah pulls me in for a hug. It feels like the last hug he'll ever give me. My throat goes tight with fear and love. He's been like my brother. It hurts to lose him, but it would hurt more to wither away in my own life. His chest hitches.

"Does he at least have one of those fancy bathrooms with the decorative towels?"

"No." A laugh bursts out of me. "His whole house burned down, remember?"

"Well, when he builds the new place, I hope there's one of those in it. For you."

"It takes a real friend to wish for a bathroom like that," I tell him.

He releases me, and the two of us step back. The distance between us seems like a thousand miles. "We'll always be friends."

"I know."

"You want me to wait for you?"

"What?" If he's asking me about Houston, then no. He can't spend his life waiting to see if I come running back. I'm not going to fail at this. "If you mean—"

He shakes his head. "For your car to get here."

"Oh. Yeah. It would be pretty awkward if you just stood inside watching me."

"Somebody has to do it," he says in a long-suffering tone. But then he grins at me, and it's the old Noah I met at the foster home. The one who snuck me food from the kitchen when it was strictly against the rules and protected me at the bus stop and everything else.

The two of us take seats at a wrought-iron patio set that's rusty all over, and I order an Uber. I think the driver's been hanging around waiting. The app says he'll be here in two minutes. It doesn't seem like enough time.

"Do you think you'll still become a social worker?" he asks.

"Yes." I really do think so. I'm not the kind of girl who spends all her time wishing anymore. I'm going to make it happen. "I'm going to do it all. College. My own practice. Everything."

"Good." The Uber pulls back into the motel parking lot. My heart pounds. This might be the last time I ever see him. Part of me is at peace with that. I never want Noah to feel like I'm rubbing this new life in his face. He stands up and hugs me again, and for the very last time, I let myself consider going back with him. Running away, right now. Get in the car, I would say. Let's go. Anywhere.

It would make him happy, but it would make me sad. The only place I want to go is to wherever Beau is.

It's time to get into the car. I open the back door and sit down, my hand on the handle. "Do you want a ride to the airport?" I can't go with him, but we could share a ride. Steal a few more minutes. "We could wait for you to get your stuff."

"I'll get the next one," he says. "Bye, Jane. Text me when you get home so I know you're safe."

He shuts the door and walks back to his motel door. As the car pulls away, he looks back over his shoulder at me and waves. I wave back. And then I'm gone.

CHAPTER EIGHTEEN

Beau Rochester

THE MEETING WITH Lauren and the FBI informant goes on longer than my patience. All I want is to get back to the inn, and back to Jane. The drive back doesn't take much time. It's still too long. I'll be glad when all these meetings are over and everything is settled. Relieved, at least. Maybe not glad, depending on how everything goes.

Marjorie's tidying the living room when I get back to the inn. Her eyes widen at my suit. "Hello, Mr. Rochester."

"Hi. Where's Jane and Paige?"

"Paige went to get ice cream with Mateo." She smooths a blanket over the back of the sofa. "Jane went out."

"Went out?"

"She didn't say where. I was about to go to

the grocery store—was there anything Paige wanted for dinner?"

"I don't think so."

Marjorie leaves, and I'm left alone in the front room. I should go change out of this damn suit, but worry squeezes at my stomach. She left without telling me. Joe could be watching her, waiting for her. He could have gotten ahold of her. He could have her right now. Why the hell am I still standing here?

I'm reaching to open the door when it opens into my face. Jane steps in. My heart races. Her hand flies to her throat. "Beau," she gasps. "What are you doing?"

"Where were you?" I reach around behind her and shut the door. Lock it. "I got home, and you were gone. I didn't know where the hell you were." I pull her into my arms, grip tight, and kiss her before she can answer. Hard. So hard it backs her up against the door. My hands go to the lines of her jaw and I look into eyes that are wide and dark and astonished. "Tell me where you were."

"I can't say anything when you're kissing me like that."

"Say it now."

"I went to see Noah."

She risked her safety to go see him. I try to

hold back a surge of jealousy and anger and fail. From the moment I saw her in the rain, I haven't wanted her to leave my side. That feeling has doubled and tripled since I sent her away, and since she came back. I don't want her out in the world, where any dirty cop could get to her. Where any old friend from Houston could talk her into—I don't even know what. Could take advantage. "What the hell did you do that for? You don't owe him anything."

Jane lifts her chin. "I owed him a conversation, so I went to his motel and had it with him. We talked. Then I came back here."

My blood pressure is so high I can feel my pulse banging at the insides of my veins. I wish she would just say it. I wish she would just say that she went there and slept with him. I wish she would tell me what the fuck actually happened in that motel room. Owing someone a conversation has to mean something other than sitting and chatting. Owing means a transaction.

I'm losing my mind.

"Beau." She doesn't pull her face out of my hands or elbow past me. No guilt creeps into her eyes. She puts her hands over mine and holds on tight. "We talked. Then I came back here."

"Nothing happened?" It comes out more like

an accusation than anything else.

Jane's lips part in shock. "Are you asking me if I—" Her anger softens almost immediately into understanding. I can feel it through her touch, in the way her hands tense and then soften on mine. I hate it. It feels like pity. It feels like being scorched, or having my head shoved under the water. "Oh," she says softly. "No wonder you don't trust people, after what happened with Emily."

All the old betrayal surges up again, thick and choking. It was worse than a slap in the face. Worse than Emily turning her back on me. If she'd walked away for anyone else, it might have been different. But Rhys? I fucking hate him. I still hate him for it. Guilt covers my hatred like the incoming tide. I hate him, but he was still my brother. He's also a part of Paige.

"Emily has nothing to do with this."

"I think she has everything to do with this. It hurt. What she did to you. It hurt, and it never stopped."

"I don't care—"

"And your brother shouldn't have done it, either. He should have known better. He wasn't a good person, but he was your brother, and if he could turn on you like that, why couldn't I?"

She's digging through the deepest parts of me and casting them aside. The whole structure's going to come down. Like the cliffs at Coach House. Eventually the rain and the waves will beat against the rock until it's all part of the sand. This thing I've been hanging on to—it's like those cliffs. But even stone can come down. Even rock is no match for the ocean.

I need more of her. I want to let it all go. I can't do it here, when anyone could walk in.

"Upstairs." I let go of Jane to point a finger at the staircase.

She goes.

I follow her.

At the top of the steps, she breaks into a run. I don't know a man on earth who could keep himself from chasing her. I'm right behind her on the way into her bedroom. The door slams shut under my hand and the sound is like the beginning of an avalanche. It's already happening. It's the sound of thick walls around my heart crumbling into a million pieces. Jane looked into my face and she saw. She understood. She saw straight through me, to all the guilt and anger and fear I've tried so hard not to feel. I don't fucking like it. I don't like this vulnerability.

She stands tall to face me at the edge of her

bed. I can't keep myself away from her. I'm on top of her like a wild thing. My hand on her throat. Kissing her harder than I did downstairs. I'm taking her. Fuck this. Fuck Noah and fuck Rhys, fuck all of them. She's mine. Jane breathes hard when I let her up for air. Her eyes glide over my clothes, my suit. She couldn't stop looking the day of the meeting. Now she lifts her hands to touch. Her fingers go to the buttons and her eyes rake over the fabric as I strip it off my shoulders. More buttons underneath, on my shirt. Jane darts her hands in to tug the hem free, but I can't let her have it. I'm so close to her, and I want her so much, and she watches me strip off these godforsaken clothes like they're nothing. They are nothing.

"Take them off."

Jane's hands go to her own clothes. Trembling now. Her shirt goes over her head. She wrestles herself out of her jeans. Every piece of cloth between me and her skin. I want it gone. I want everything gone.

"Nothing happened." This time it's not a question. This time, I'm trying to convince myself.

"I only want you."

I want to believe her so badly. I want to believe her with everything I have, but there's a small, hidden part of me that doesn't. I believed Emily, and it was a lie. Everything turned out not to be true. Jane's naked, her eyes huge, lips parted. Panting. She lets me scare her, and then she lets me bend her over the bed.

I push into her without any more hesitation. I've been waiting all goddamn day. I've been waiting all my life. Jane's hands fist in the blankets and she makes a sound like I'm hurting her, like it's almost too much. But she doesn't stand up. She doesn't tell me to stop. Doesn't push me away.

None of that. She spreads her thighs for me and angles herself back to take more of me. I thrust into her like an animal. My hands circle the bones of her hips and hold her down so she can't escape.

"Yes," she whispers. "Please."

"No more." No more of Noah. No more of the past. Those things are gone now. Done. I'm not going back to that fear and that betrayal. It's not happening again with Jane. It won't. "You're mine."

Another thrust knocks the breath out of her. "I want to stay."

"Then stay. Don't ever fucking leave. Don't

leave again." I bend down over her and write it on the back of her neck with the tip of my tongue. S-T-A-Y-S-T-A-Y-S-T-A-Y. She's slick around me. Tight. I didn't give her time to be ready. I didn't lick her until she was squirming. I took her like this because I thought she might not let me. She might fight, she might run. She might be like every other good thing in my life. S-T-A-Y. Jane clenches around me and buries her face in the covers. I put my fingers in her hair and pull her face up.

"I want to hear you. I want to hear everything."

She whimpers, needy, and I hear what she wants in that sound. I've made my point. She's mine, she's mine.

I turn her onto her back and crawl over her. Jane throws her arms around my neck and I find the wet seam of her with my fingers. Toy with her. Her body is all movement under mine. Movement and soft skin. "Tell me what you need. It's yours. It's all yours."

I'm talking about sex. I'm talking about money. I'm talking about everything in the whole damn world. Everything I have is hers. All the old hurts and the danger that stalks under my skin. All of it.

"I need you." Jane's breath catches. My thumb on her clit makes it catch again. "I need you everywhere. Inside me. Everywhere."

She rocks her hips until she finds me. Takes me in. Envelops me completely. I bend to kiss her. O-N-L-Y-Y-O-U, I write into her mouth, into her body, with every thrust, with everything. Jane Mendoza could have gone anywhere, but she came back to me. S-T-A-Y.

Jane moves with me, seeking contact and pressure, and when she comes, her body squeezes mine in a tight grip. I surrender myself to it. My orgasm arrives like a wave on rock, cracking open. She kisses the line of my jaw while it happens. "Yes," she whispers in my ear. "I can feel you."

I can feel her. Every brave heartbeat. Every gentle touch. They're all I've ever wanted from anyone, and they're here in this one woman, this perfect person. She could have run away from me. She should have stayed in Houston. But she's with me now. I roll off her, onto the sheets, and bring her with me.

"I'm staying," she whispers.

CHAPTER NINETEEN

Beau Rochester

DINNER HAPPENS LATE and in the kind of chaos that can only happen when you've eaten too much ice cream, which Paige has. She tears tiny pieces off her grilled cheese and dips them in ketchup, but she won't eat most of it.

"I'm done," she says finally.

"Okay," Jane says. She picks up Paige's plate and takes it over to the sink. I would do anything to take her back to bed. That's where I plan to go the instant Paige is asleep.

The knock at the door is loud and persistent. Jane drops the plate into the sink. Ceramic meets the stainless steel and cracks. "It broke," Jane says. She glances over her shoulder at me.

Another knock. This one louder. Like someone's trying to break the damn door down. Marjorie's out for the night. A book club—

something like that. We're on our own. Jane peers out the window over the kitchen sink. "I see lights out there."

They're everywhere in the yard. Red and blue. Police.

We both react at the same time. Jane comes across the room to meet me. Paige scrambles down from her chair and flies to Jane's side. "What's going on?"

The three of us go through into the inn's living area.

"Take her upstairs," I tell Jane.

"No." Paige plants her feet on the floor. I can hear the resistance in her tone. The way she's absolutely not going to do this. I should have had Mateo stay here until everything was finished. "I'm not going upstairs."

"It's a good idea to go upstairs," Jane coaxes. But we both know what it means if the police come to the door.

"Police," says a voice from the outside, and my stomach sinks. The last hope that it was someone, anyone, other than Joe—it's gone now. Joe's outside the door. I make a split-second decision. I can't let Paige watch him break down the door, which he'll do if he doesn't get his way. She'll never feel safe in the house again. I'll have to stop him myself.

So I open it. "Not tonight. If you want an interview—"

He shoves me out of the way and stalks through to the living room. I go with him, trying to keep myself between him and everything that matters to me in the world. Joe's eyes are wild. Bright.

"I have a warrant." He pushes the paper into my face, too fast for me to read any of it. Adrenaline bursts across my vision in reds and blacks. I put both hands on him and push him back. He looks down at my hands on his shirt. A sneer curls the corner of his mouth.

"Go back out. This isn't the way to do this."

"I said I have a warrant, Rochester." The lights of his cruiser flash outside, but no other cops come in behind him. I don't like this brightness in his eyes. I don't like his uneven breathing. He's snapped. He's come here to finish all this, and he doesn't care if it's by the book. The warrant is only a cover for what he's planning to do. "I'm taking you both. This stupid fucking game is over. You're both done."

I back him up another few steps, but he resists. I'm going to take him all the way outside. Drag him into the ocean and drown him.

Whatever it takes.

"Beau. Stop." Jane wraps both her hands around my arms. "Get away from him. Listen to me. You can't touch him. You have to let go of him."

"You stay away from her." I won't back down from Joe Causey. Not now. "You don't touch her. You shouldn't be here, Causey."

"This is exactly where I should be. You thought you could get away with this. You can't, Rochester. It's over."

"Beau. Please. Don't touch him anymore. Don't." Her voice shakes. "He could hurt you," she says, pitching her voice low, and it finally dawns on me what she's so afraid of. Joe came in here with his weapons. He could shoot me now and say I was resisting arrest. He could say anything, and the department might believe him, investigation be damned. And if I die in front of Jane and Paige, it won't matter if they find him guilty. I'll be dead.

I back off a few steps. "If you take one step toward Jane, I'll kill you."

Joe's eyes glitter. This is what he wanted me to say. "Fine with me."

A fight to the death with Joe won't just mean that I die. He could kill Jane and Paige, too.

Paige—

I twist around to make sure she's okay and find her hiding behind Jane, her eyes like saucers. She looks so young. Too young to be in the middle of a scene like this.

"I'm putting you both under arrest," Joe says. "For arson."

"You can't do that," says Jane.

"Did you not hear? I have a warrant, Ms. Mendoza. For your arrest. That means I can handcuff you right now and take you into custody. In fact, that's exactly what's going to happen."

This is why I sent her away. To save her. And I failed. I failed. I let her come back, and I didn't protect her, and now this asshole is standing in here threatening the both of us. The three of us. All the meetings have come to nothing. It's nothing if he puts his hands on her. And he's going to.

It's going to be all fucking wrong. He came in here brandishing a warrant, but he didn't read us our rights. He's way off script. There's no telling how this ends. The gun on his belt heightens everything.

"I'm going to need you to come this way." Joe puts a hand to the cuffs on his belt. He's slipping into his usual cop bullshit. "Right now, Ms. Mendoza."

Jane's not having this. "I'm not going with you. I won't leave Paige alone. And I—I want a lawyer."

Joe laughs. "You can contact your representation after you've been processed. Step to this side of the room."

"No."

He moves toward her, his mouth set in a line. "You'll also be charged for resisting arrest and obstruction of justice. Why not throw in assaulting an officer?"

This isn't happening. My blood sears my veins, setting every single one of them on fire, and I put myself between them again. She begged me not to, but I'm not letting him put his hands on her. Not Joe. Not anyone. Not ever again. "Don't touch her. You want to talk about this, we'll go outside and talk. There's not going to be any arrest until we have a conversation."

"Step aside."

Paige starts to cry. A thin wail goes up into the middle of the room, and I'm done. I'm done with this fucked-up situation. He's not doing this to Paige. She's been through enough already. "I want him to leave," she sobs. "I want him to leave."

I'm going to kill him. Crime or not. Charges or not. This ends now. Jane's hands tighten on my arm. Joe's about to move around me. He's already reaching, like he's going to touch her arm, but he's not going to do that. No one is ever going to touch her again. It's the moment before a match meets kindling. Everything roars into flame.

I'm a single breath from murdering a police officer when the front door of the inn opens again.

Everyone in the room freezes, like we've all been caught in the act.

Emily steps into the room. She takes in the scene. Me, about to kill her brother. Joe, about to put his hands on Jane. "Enough," she says, her voice clear. "It's not them you want. It's me."

I don't see Paige move, but I feel it. She's moving too fast for me to catch her with one hand. She darts out from behind Jane, from behind me, her chest heaving.

"Paige," Emily says.

"Mommy," Paige screams, and she sprints across the room to her.

My heart breaks in two at the sight of her running toward Emily. Emily kneels down on the floor to catch Paige in her arms, and Paige barrels into her at full speed. It almost knocks them both to the ground, but Emily catches the child against her body. I see her face as her arms go around her daughter for the first time in months. It's sheer relief.

"It's okay," she murmurs. "It's okay. I'm here."

"You died," Paige wails. "You died. You weren't coming back. Beau said you were never coming back."

"I did come back. I did." Emily scans the room. The rest of us are still frozen in this hellish moment. I see realization come to her eyes. She pulls Paige into a tighter squeeze. "Joe," she says, her tone even. "Did you come here alone?"

He grins. "I had unfinished business."

CHAPTER TWENTY

Jane Mendoza

EMILY'S QUESTION EXPLODES the tension in the room.

Did you come here alone?

I had unfinished business.

"Get the hell out, Causey." Beau is yelling, at his full height, trying to back Joe to the door. "You know this isn't right. You know you're going down for this."

It's wrong to have all this shouting and tension in the inn. This is a place where people come for peace, not to threaten each other. Marjorie's carefully chosen furniture makes the argument building between the two men more horrifying. The space looks fragile around them. All those spindly table legs could break in an instant if things escalated.

From the way my pulse feels, it's going to

escalate past all reason. I don't know who's going to get out of this unscathed. None of us, probably. Whatever happens tonight will follow us all into the future. I can't bring myself to think of all the different paths it could take.

I want to run between the two of them and demand they stop, but making a sudden movement near Joe Causey seems like the worst of all worlds. I'd never forgive myself if I set him off and something happened to Paige. So I stay where I am.

"I'm here to arrest a couple of fucking criminals," Joe spits back at him. "You and your whore nanny."

"You're not doing this." Beau gets him another few feet to the door. It looks difficult. Joe came here with his mind made up. There's only one more obstacle in front of him.

"I have the warrant, and I have the rights, and it's time for this to come to an end. You've lived outside the law for too long now, Rochester." What is he talking about? Joe's the one who's been outside the law. It strikes me that he might be more than a little delusional. He might have twisted this all around in his mind so he's the hero. There's no other way he could be justifying this.

"I don't believe you. I haven't been able to read it. Why the hell isn't anyone here with you?"

"I'm in charge of this case."

"You're not in any state of mind to be doing this. You've entered a home with women and children in it and you're acting like a goddamn menace. You want any of us to go with you, you get on your phone right now and call the prosecutor."

"I'm not going to do that. You're going to—"

Beau reaches into his pocket and takes out his phone. "I'll call her, then. I want to know what the hell is happening, and why the entire police department agreed to send you."

And that's when Joe reaches for his gun. Levels it at Beau. "Drop it."

Beau throws the phone disgustedly into a corner of the room and puts his hands out in front of him. "You're afraid of a phone call now? I thought you had a warrant." He's still moving, just slower. Angling Joe away from Emily and Paige. She ducks down and hustles Paige behind him, their footsteps light. We're still close enough for Joe to shoot.

"Put the gun away," Beau demands. He does it in the tone of a man who gets what he wants. Who wears fancy suits to meetings and can afford to buy anything he wants. "Paige is in here."

Joe's eyes go to the three of us, and indecision comes into his expression. No matter how this ends, it's going badly for him. He just pulled a gun on Beau, who doesn't have one, and two women, and a child. "I'm not done here. I have a warrant, and that's the end of the line for you."

"Put the damn thing away."

Joe Causey hesitates for another few seconds. My heart races and pounds. It's all I can hear in this room. My own heartbeat. The gun goes down an inch, then another. He's deciding whether to shoot Beau, I can tell. He's still deciding whether he's going to do this.

I might be seconds away from watching Beau die. I'm afraid to breathe.

Joe lowers the gun another few inches. His arm flexes. He's going to put it away. If he would just let go of it, I would feel better. It would give us a little time. A few seconds, at least, to figure out what to do.

It's an inch away from the holster when his eyes darken. "No," he says, and he starts to bring it back up.

Beau jumps toward him, swinging, fighting, and I can't understand a word either of them is saying. Curses and shouts. Beside me, Paige has

Emily's coat in a death grip. We end up by the kitchen door, Emily kneeling down, working hard to detach her daughter's nails from her coat. She pushes us fully into the kitchen, but it's not far enough. We're blocked by the door. If Joe's gun goes off, it probably won't hit us, but if Paige breaks and runs—

"This only ends if I do this," she says, and I realize after a beat that she's talking to me. "You have to take her."

"Emily. No."

"Paige." Emily takes her baby's face in her hands and looks into her eyes. Her entire expression transforms. There's no fear in it now, only seriousness. Only love. "You need to go with Jane now. Okay? You have to stay with her in the kitchen."

A lamp crashes to the ground. Paige has stopped making any noise but she's crying. Her little shoulders shake. My chest feels like it's about to implode from the pressure. I can't see what Beau's hands are doing. The light from the kitchen makes them into shadows.

I reach down and take Paige's hand. I'll keep her out of the way, but I'm not letting Emily walk out of here with Joe. She'll be dead before they get to his car. He's willing to do it.

"No," Paige says, and her face goes a deep scarlet. "No."

In this situation, I won't be able to convince her to calm down. There won't be any way to redirect her from this meltdown. My heart aches for Emily. This is not the reunion she dreamed about with Paige—it can't be.

"Stay here." Emily leans in and kisses her cheek. "I'll be back in just a minute."

"No," Paige screams, but Emily tears herself away.

Paige throws herself into the fight and I get my arms around her in time to keep her from running after Emily. She's battling me with everything she has. Sharp elbows. Stomping feet. Her howls block out all the other noise in the room. This is too much for a little girl. It's too much for anyone. I try to move her into the kitchen, but she digs her heels in, slapping one hand on the doorframe. She's determined to go back out there. She doesn't know, or doesn't understand, how dangerous this is. I can't blame her. In the space of one evening our lives have spun out of control.

Emily is in the fray now, saying something to Joe. Something loud. "—go with you."

"No," I tell her. *She can't leave her daughter again.*

Joe turns his head. He's distracted. One hand reaches away from his gun and toward her. Emily leans in, as if she's going to let him do it. As if she's going to let him drag her out of here by her arm and kill her.

That's the opening Beau needs. He puts an arm across Joe's chest and they're wrestling again, only this time Emily is there, too. All her focus is on the gun. Getting it out of Joe's hands. A flash of metal in the kitchen light. Paige's screams are even louder now, filled with the same helplessness and rage I feel. It's taking all my strength to keep her with me. I understand. I'd rather be out there, too. It would be better than standing on the sidelines and waiting for all this violence to determine the rest of our lives.

Emily stumbles back. "I have it," she says. "I have it."

It's too much for Joe. His rage overtakes him. His eyes lock on Emily and the gun in her hands. This desperate plan was his only chance to fix things for himself. He's a big man, and in his anger he seems even bigger. But he's too wild. He doesn't have the presence of mind to coordinate himself against Beau Rochester.

Beau manhandles him to the front door of the inn and wrenches it open. He pushes Joe out onto the porch. The front yard is flooded with lights. Joe's silhouetted against miles and miles of red and blue. I see him shift, one direction, then the other. Deciding whether to run.

There's nowhere to go. They have the whole yard surrounded, and then there are men thundering up onto the porch. Cracking footsteps thunder on old wood. Black FBI jackets crowd around Joe. My lungs scream for air, and I finally take a breath.

Paige wrenches from my hands and sprints toward Emily. She holds the gun up high, chest level, like she's trying to keep it above water. "Beau," she calls. He's the closest one to her. He takes the gun from her hands and unloads it, tipping brass into his hand.

A lone agent walks into the living room. All the flashing lights make this place look like a movie set, but it's real. It's happening. My heart is going crazy. Beau hands over the gun and the bullets.

In a minute, all this activity is going to bubble over into the room. Into the inn. Someone will turn on all the lights. They might bring more lights—I don't know. For now, Emily stands next to Beau. She leans down and picks up Paige, who wraps herself around her mom. Emily guides

Paige's head to her shoulder with one hand and whispers to her. I feel a pang of jealousy. They look good together, even bathed in red and blue like this. The three of them would be beautiful in a family portrait.

Beau looks at Emily holding Paige.

And then he looks at me.

The jealousy disappears like a popped bubble. His dark eyes settle on mine. I feel the same heat I did in the bedroom earlier. The same possession. We could be standing anywhere on the face of the earth, and it would feel just like this for him to look at me.

He holds out his hand, and I go to him.

Beau's tall and solid, and I slide my hands around his waist and hold on tight. He folds his arms around me. The heat of him creates a barrier between me and the world. I would be fine if we went upstairs right now and collapsed into bed. I would be more than fine if we never did anything like this again. If I never watched him fight off a cop with a gun again. His big hands move up and down over my back. "Are you okay?" he asks. I feel the words through his chest more than I hear them. It's loud in here. The voices from outside echo in and overlap with one another.

I am now.

CHAPTER TWENTY-ONE

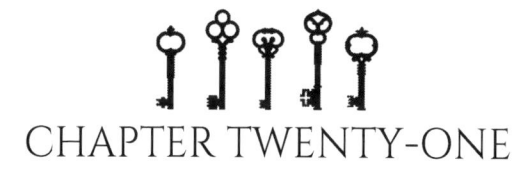

Beau Rochester

FBI AGENTS ARE all over the inn. Marjorie pulls up while they're in full force, taking pictures and collecting evidence. She walks up the sidewalk, staring at the inn. "What happened?" she asks, her hand dropping to the side. Her purse dangles from her fingertips. "I just went to book club."

"We had a visit from Joe Causey."

"Joe Causey and the FBI?"

"Yeah."

Marjorie shakes her head. "Is everybody okay?"

"Nobody got hurt."

Joe got a black eye. He also got arrested. And I have a pain around my heart that has nothing to do with the physical fight.

When Emily walked Paige out of the inn to

give the FBI agents room to do their jobs, it was like Paige came to after a long sleep. She took one look into Emily's face and demanded to be let go. Then she ran into Jane's arms. She hasn't let go of her since then. The two of them sit on a blanket on the lawn, Paige clinging to Jane and watching all the action with suspicion in her eyes. Kitten cowers in her lap. She streaked out of the inn behind everyone else. Hid the whole fight. Emily stands nearby, her hands in her pockets and longing in her eyes.

"I couldn't find a parking spot." Marjorie laughs weakly. "There are so many cars on the road that I couldn't find a spot."

"I'm sure they'll be gone soon. And I hope you know I'll pay extra for all the trouble."

She waves this off. "You don't have to do that, Beau."

"I think I do. This has been a mess since we first moved in."

Marjorie lets out a breath. She knows I'm right. There hasn't been a moment of peace since we descended on this place. Paige almost brought the whole place down on us with her screaming that very first night. And now there are FBI agents everywhere. It's an official crime scene. Camera flashes go off inside. Lauren stands on the porch in a navy jacket, talking to the men in there.

This quiet seaside inn has made all kinds of sacrifices for us.

"Is that Emily?" Marjorie's eyes go wide with disbelief. "Emily?" she says, louder.

Emily gives her a little wave. They were friends before. Not best friends or anything, but friends. Marjorie forgets all about me and goes to talk to her. Emily doesn't look quite ready for this. She takes a step back as Marjorie arrives and throws her arms around her for a quick embrace.

"Beau." Lauren Michaels steps to my side along with the FBI agent in charge of all this. "I wanted to keep you updated. We've got the footage from the security cameras, and I've had two people from my team review them independently."

"Good news for me, I hope."

"Yeah. It is." Lauren glances back toward the inn. "The place has been turned upside down, but we'll be able to use the evidence to keep Causey behind bars while he awaits trial. Oh, we also found evidence that he's the one who left the rat."

"The trial. How long's that going to take?" I don't like the thought of him being released into the world under any circumstance. Jane and Paige and Emily don't deserve that.

She shrugs. "Depends. The trial can't start until we've got a jury together, but it'll be a tough sell in Eben Cape. Too many people know him." Lauren looks me in the eye. "You've got time."

I watch the FBI agents moving in front of the open door. They do it with purpose. Jane and Paige and I—we were in over our heads when we got here. It's a miracle Marjorie didn't kick us out after the first week. I wouldn't have blamed her if she did.

Okay, I would have blamed her. But I would have understood.

"How's everybody doing?" Lauren asks. "Emily looks pretty good."

Actually, Emily doesn't look good. She looks worried. It's obviously hard for her to stop looking at Paige. After their brief reunion inside, I'm not sure when she's going to get another one. "Everybody's pretty shaken up," I admit. "You saw the video."

"Yeah." Lauren pats my arm. "You need anything, you can always call me. You know that, right? Any of you."

"I do. Thank you."

She goes back to her job. What's a person supposed to do when the FBI is in the goddamn inn he rented? I don't want to hover over Jane and Paige. I don't want to follow the agents around in some kind of weird job shadow. I just want to be sure that we're all safe.

And for the first time since Rhys died and Emily disappeared, I'm pretty sure we are.

Joe Causey was driven away in a cruiser by some of the first agents on the scene. I trust Lauren's word about keeping him behind bars until the trial. I also know she's right about the jury. Eben Cape is full of people who will have an opinion about Joe. Some of them will believe that because he's an officer, he's within his rights to do just about goddamn anything. Others will remember what an asshole he was in school.

We've got time.

Which is good, because we're going to need it. Paige is going to have to get over the shock of Emily's return. All kinds of emotion are going to come with that. It's already been a hell of a year. And Jane—

We'll have to work things out, too. We've been in survival mode for a long time. It's going to be different when it's just real life. Day in. Day out. There's a house to be rebuilt, or not be rebuilt. There are decisions to make about Paige. There will be more to do with Joe Causey, though at least we won't have to see him in person.

Groceries and homework and what to do about college for Jane.

"Beau," Marjorie calls. She gestures for me to come over and join them, so I do. There's nothing to keep watch over in the middle of the yard. "One of the men—the agents—he said they're going to be clearing out in the next couple of minutes. We can go back inside."

Paige won't let go of Jane to let her stand up from the ground. I take her hand and help her up. Paige keeps her face turned away from Emily. I see pain flicker across Emily's face, but she doesn't say anything. Things between Emily and Paige—those will take time, too. Emily never wanted to leave her daughter. It must have torn her apart to be away from Paige for so long. It'll all look different from Paige's point of view.

"Maybe I should go," Emily suggests.

"No," Jane says. "We'll all go inside together."

Emily's eyebrows go up. She looks at me for confirmation. What am I going to do, send her back to that A-frame in the woods? "Come in with us," I agree. "We'll have some tea."

"Hot chocolate," Paige says, her demand sounding almost automatic.

Jane smooths her hair back from her face. "Hot chocolate sounds good," she says. Emily looks away. As painful as it must have been to be separated, this would also cause a new kind of pain.

The FBI agents start leaving. It's a coordinated departure. They leave together the way they came. One of the agents hands me a slip of paper on the way out. "For the cameras," he says. "We have to take them in to transfer the footage to our systems, but you can have them back when we're done."

I don't know what to say to that, so I just nod at him.

Jane goes through the door ahead of me, Paige tucked to her side, and I follow them.

CHAPTER TWENTY-TWO

Jane Mendoza

THINGS ARE PRETTY awkward after all the FBI agents leave.

We go into the inn and take seats in the living room, which is all wrong. Somehow they managed to move most of the furniture, but only a few inches out of place. Marjorie moves at superhuman speed through the room to put it back together. Bit by bit, she straightens it up around us. Enough that I can sit in a big armchair with Paige. Emily and Beau sit on the couch. Kitten jumps into my lap, then out of it, then finally settles on one of the nearby couch cushions.

"I heard Paige wants hot chocolate," Marjorie says as she bustles toward the kitchen. "Anyone else?"

"Coffee," says Beau.

Emily doesn't want anything, and neither do I. What I want to do is pull the covers over me in bed and sleep all the adrenaline off. It's already fleeing from my veins. I'm tired, but still too hyped up to sleep.

Marjorie brings hot chocolate. Paige takes a few sips and hands it to me.

"Lauren says he'll be kept in custody until the trial," Beau mentions.

"That's good," answers Emily.

Paige is staring at her. After the way she chased her before, I'd thought she'd spend the rest of the evening in Emily's arms.

"She'll be in contact with us throughout the process," Beau says. He looks into his coffee as he says it. I have no idea what time it is. Late enough that Paige should be in bed. But this is the first time we've been able to sit down together. The incident we just went through doesn't lend itself to a peaceful bedtime routine. "If you want me to have her call you, too, I can."

"That would be good." Emily glances at the door, then back at Paige. I can see the indecision in her face. She thinks she should leave, but she wants to stay.

I can feel the anxiety coming off of Paige's small body. Her own indecision is as palpable as

Emily's. I hope she doesn't regret going to her before. I hope she doesn't think I wanted to keep them apart. If I'm hoping it, she might be wondering, so I wrap my arms around her and lean down to speak into her ear.

"It's okay if you want to go sit with your mom," I say.

Paige looks at me, blue eyes glimmering with tears. "I want to sit with her."

"I think she wants to sit with you, too. It's okay. Go."

Her wavering doesn't last. Paige leans against me, a quick hug, and then she bounds across the living room and tosses herself onto the couch between Emily and Beau. Her hands go out and she pulls them both in. All the tension files out of the room like a departing FBI agent. "Hi, baby," Emily says. And then she looks at Beau over Paige's head. They're squished together on the couch, Paige connecting them. "Thank you. For taking care of her."

He tries to wave it off.

Emily won't have it. "I mean it, Beau. I know—I know it had to be hard." She's stroking Paige's hair now, the movement natural and familiar. She probably missed those tiny things more than anything. "Burying Rhys, and then the two of you together, all alone. I couldn't have asked for a better person to step in. I'm going to owe you for the rest of my life."

"You don't owe me." His voice is gruff. A moment of silence passes. "I'm sorry. For not intervening with Rhys. I knew what kind of person he was, and I should have made a point of seeing if you were okay. I regret it."

"It's over," Emily whispers. There's a complicated relief in her voice. "That's all over now. I don't hold any of that against you."

I feel like a statue. Part of the furniture. I don't want them to look at me, or notice me—I don't want this moment for myself. It belongs completely to Beau and Emily, and to Paige, who has her mom back. It's what she's wanted most in the world. I'm so happy for her my heart could burst. I'm happy, and so, so sad.

"Just wanted you to know," Beau says. He looks like a weight has been taken off his shoulders. His regret has been a physical burden for a long time. He never felt right about sleeping with Emily behind Rhys's back. He never felt right that his brother had died. Never felt right about any of it. Saying the words to Emily seems to heal some of that for him.

Paige pulls up her legs and sticks them across

Beau's lap. I think she might fall asleep like that. He glances down at Paige, and then he smiles at Emily.

They're such a nice family.

My heart cracks. I get up quietly, so quietly that I don't distract them. I keep my footsteps soft on the way up to my room. I push the door so it's almost closed, leaving it open a crack.

And then I press both hands to my chest and try to stop the pain.

They're such a nice family, down there on the couch. They belong together. Beautiful Emily. Beautiful Beau. Beautiful Paige. They came from this place, and they're meant to be here together. I feel like I'm falling through the floor of the inn.

I can't take that away from them. That means I can't have Beau. I definitely can't have Paige. Paige doesn't need a nanny now that she has Emily back. It's true that my contract with Beau is technically terminated, but I had the idea that I would stay for Paige. How could I have thought that? Emily's going to take her back. It's right for a girl to be with her mom. That leaves no place for me.

I try to picture it. Living in Beau's house and watching them being a happy family. Emily's voice in the kitchen in the mornings. The three of them walking on the beach. Paige showing off her new sandcastles. A mom, a dad, a daughter. There's no room in that scenario for a nanny who used to sleep with her boss.

They're such a nice family. They're going to be so perfect together. So happy. Who am I to choose anything else? No one. Jane Mendoza from Houston.

I'm leaving.

As soon as the decision is made, I find the will to stand up and head for the dresser. My carry-on suitcase is on top. I unpacked it, but I never put it into the closet. It's a narrow closet in this room and the suitcase sticks on the door every time. I toss it on the bed. Good decision-making on my part. If the suitcase got stuck in the closet door right now, I think I'd sit down and cry.

There's not much to pack but I can't bring myself to do it too quickly. The clothes I threw into the dresser are mostly unfolded. I've spent every minute since I got here with Beau or with Paige. I've barely thought about my clothes. Only keeping our heads above water.

It's over.

Where am I going to go?

Not back to Houston.

I fold a pair of yoga pants and put them into

the suitcase.

It seems like the obvious choice, going back to Houston. It's what I know. Maybe it's even the smartest thing, to go back to a place I know. But I'm certain of one thing, and it's that my old life won't work for me. I'll never go back to the old apartment with my roommates. I could find somewhere else to live in the city, but that would mean explaining it to Noah.

It would mean admitting to him that I should have made a different choice.

I'm not going to admit it to him, and I'm not going to admit it to myself. I made the right choice. It was absolutely right to come back here with Emily. It was the only way this tangle of past wrongs could be fixed.

A shirt goes into the suitcase. It's almost meditative, the folding and the smoothing. This is how a person prepares for a new life. She arranges her things in a way that will survive the trip. The fabric feels good in my hands. It's all expensive. Everything Beau bought me. I said I'd pay him back and I never did. That'll have to wait, too. Until I can make some money of my own. I'll need a job.

In the end, all of this means I'll still need a degree. In-state schools are cheaper, but there's no requirement I go back to Houston. I could go anywhere, enroll in community college, and stay for as long as it takes to get residency. Then—

Then—

I'm going to miss him every day. No matter where I go. I'm going to miss Beau so much I can hardly breathe. I already miss him, and he's just downstairs. I'm going to miss Paige. I'm going to miss this glimmer of a new life I had with them both.

Kitten pads into the room and winds herself around my ankles. I'm going to miss her, too. She'll be all grown up soon. I reach down and pat her soft fur. Her heartbeat thrums underneath her skin. They'll all move on without me. I won't be missing from their lives in the same way they'll be missing from mine.

That's okay. I try to tell myself that it's okay. I try to comfort myself with the things we used to say in the foster home, Noah and I. That nothing is permanent. We're just on our way somewhere else. This too shall pass.

This ache I have for Beau—it won't go away. I'm going to have to learn to live with it.

I can't decide if I want to go somewhere harsh and cold and unrelenting so that the weather consumes me, or somewhere absolutely beautiful so that I can never have to think about it. Ironically, the one place I want to stay is Eben Cape. It felt so unfamiliar when I got here. I was all wrong for it, and I thought I'd never fit in. But now I'm dressed for the occasion. I have everything I need to make a life here except a good reason to stay.

Ruining a beautiful family is not a good reason to stay.

Another shirt into the suitcase. I break the trip down into small pieces. I'll need an Uber to the airport, and then a plane ticket. One thing I've never done, one thing I've never had the money to do, is to decide on a random destination when I'm already at the airport. Only rich people get to do that.

I have the money. It's waiting for me. If I'm doing this, if I'm going to give Beau and Emily and Paige the happiness they deserve, then it takes the guilt away from using some of the money for me.

That's what I'll do.

I'll finish packing my suitcase. Everything will be neat and tidy and ready to go. I'll call an Uber. I'll slip out while they're putting Paige to bed. I'll have him drive me to the airport and I'll choose from all the available destinations. There might be a wait, a long stretch with an airport coffee and a magazine I won't read, but the waiting is part of the process. It's when you let all your expectations go.

The plane will arrive, and the attendant will check my ticket, and I won't be alone, not really. There will be other people around me as I walk down the jetway to the plane. I'll find my seat. I'll stow my luggage. I'll let myself think of Beau and Paige one more time and hope they're not thinking of me. I hope they won't miss me. I'll hope they'll be so happy that I never cross their minds.

And then I'll fly away.

CHAPTER TWENTY-THREE
Emily Rochester

I HAVE MY daughter in my arms again. She clings to me, curling into my lap, and what else am I supposed to care about? Everything, I suppose. A previously dead woman can't hang out in an inn that she's not renting.

Jane stands up and slips out of the room. Beau's eyes stay on Paige. Maybe that was some kind of signal they arranged. That it's time for me to go. Paige closes her eyes and relaxes. I could cry, but that would drip tears all over her face and wake her up. I missed this so much. I missed everything about her so much.

"I should go," I hear myself say. I'm right. I should go, and leave Paige with Beau and Jane until everything is worked out. No one can make any decisions after a night like this one.

"There's plenty of room here," Beau says.

"Paige will want to see you in the morning."

Will she? She'd have every right to wake up angry at me for leaving her. And then for showing up without any warning. "Are you sure?"

Beau has spent more time with her over the past months than I have. He would know. As much as it hurts.

"You're her mom. She'll want to see you." He's so firm about it, the way he was firm about everything.

"What about you? Are you sure you want me to stay?" I'm obviously interrupting something. Beau and Jane have a way to be together, and I'm barging into the middle of it. Staying at the inn doesn't make it any easier.

"I'm sure." Beau stands. "Do you want me to carry her up?"

"No. Thanks." I don't want her away from me. Not tonight. I rub Paige's shoulder and her eyes pop open. "Let's get ready for bed."

Upstairs in Paige's bedroom, I go through her dresser and find a pair of pajamas. Everything is brand new and soft. She doesn't have anything left from when Coach House burned. Nothing I recognize. Nothing I bought. Paige allows me to slip the shirt over her head and hold out the shorts to step into, even though she's old enough to do it herself. She lets me run a brush through her hair and put toothpaste on her toothbrush.

She lets me tuck her into bed.

These motions, these actions—they're bone-deep in my memory. So deep my hands shake. I have to hide it from Paige. Putting toothpaste on a child-sized toothbrush is one of those monotonous things that you take for granted until you don't get to do it anymore. Paige used to fight with me about the toothpaste. She'd insist on doing it herself. It would always end up all over her little hands, and the sink. She would fight with me, but I never tried to stop her.

"Lie with me?" she asks when I reach to turn out the lamp. A small nightlight flares to life in the corner of the room.

"Of course I will." It's a twin bed, not very big, but Paige is still small enough that we both fit. My heart hurts. The months I missed were too long, but they could have been years and years. I was so close to losing her forever.

Paige presses her body to my side and cuddles. A few tears drip down my cheek, but I keep my breathing steady. I don't want her to think I'm sad about this. Nervous, maybe. Apprehensive about how things will go with Beau and Jane now that I'm here. But I'm not sad.

"I missed you so much," Paige whispers, her voice breaking.

"I missed you too." I kiss her hair, breathe her in. She smells like shampoo and sunshine. I can still remember how she smelled the day she was born, all downy and soft and so, so good. "I missed you every single day."

"I thought you were alive," she says. "I knew you were and nobody would believe me about it. I saw you outside."

That makes a lump rise to my throat. I didn't think Paige would see me when I walked on the beach. I never wanted her to think that I left her. It was a weakness of mine. When I climbed out of the water the night Rhys was killed, I promised myself I'd stay away from Paige until I was sure it was safe.

I couldn't keep that promise. I missed her like I'd miss my own heart, or my lungs. I missed her so much my skin hurt. I felt the weight of her in my arms as a baby and as a little girl. The first day I dropped her off at preschool, she stood in the corner of the room. Paige was still red-faced and stubborn when I got back. I stepped into the room, and she ran to me, tears running down her face.

After all that, she claimed it was a great day.

"I was alive," I tell her. "You were right."

There's a long pause. "Is Daddy still alive?"

"No, sweetheart, he's not."

Another pause. Paige rubs at her eyes. I expect anger and tears, but she just settles against me again. "Are you still scared of him?"

I don't know what to say. My lungs feel frozen now. I didn't realize she knew how I felt about Rhys. Shit. If she knows I was scared of him, she might have understood much more than I knew. My instinct is to shush her, to brush it off, to tell her we won't talk about it. But she knows. She was there.

"I'm not still scared of him," I say carefully. "He's gone now. He died, and he's not coming back."

"Because he made you cry."

"No, that's—that's not why he's gone. There was an accident." The accident was my brother going out of his mind, but that hardly seems age-appropriate to tell Paige. "He died because of the accident. It's also true that Daddy was not a good man, and he did hurt Mommy."

"I saw him doing that."

Damn you, Rhys.

"Beau's grumpy," Paige says into the new silence. "He can't make grilled cheese, but Jane can, so you don't have to worry about that."

"I don't?"

"No." She yawns. "We're going to have so much fun together. We can go to the beach and build sandcastles. And if you get hungry, Jane can make you a grilled cheese."

Shit. Beau and Jane have built a family for Paige. Not just a temporary shelter, but a real family. She expects them to be there for her.

"Mommy?"

"Yeah?"

"Do you not like grilled cheese?"

"I love grilled cheese." Actually I haven't thought about grilled cheese in months. I would only ever make it for Paige and eat the crusts she didn't want.

"Do you like our kitten?"

"The kitten's very cute."

Paige is growing heavy against my side. When she was first outgrowing her crib and moving to a bigger bed, it was impossible for her to sleep alone. I spent lots of nights waiting for her to fall asleep. We'd read book after book, and she would close her eyes, but then she'd pop back up again and tell me something else.

I never wanted to leave her room afterward. Or—really, I wanted to leave her room and go outside to a peaceful home. One where my volatile husband wasn't downstairs in his office, waiting for me. I'd lie in bed next to Paige and daydream about reading a book in my own bed until my eyes closed. Waking up to a quiet house before it was time to take her to school. It never seemed possible while Rhys was alive. I knew he'd make a divorce ugly and probably dangerous. He'd spend his money to ruin me, and there would be no explaining it to Paige.

So I stayed.

I waited until she fell asleep.

And then I went downstairs and tried to keep him in a good mood.

"I'm allergic to shellfish," Paige murmurs sleepily.

"I know," I tell her. "You always got a rash."

She doesn't answer. My daughter is asleep now. I'm wide awake. In the darkness of her room, I look at the outline of the window and worry. I'm too tired to be awake, but now my mind is racing like my heart.

I left Paige behind to keep her safe. What if that's the answer now? All over again? What if the best place for her is with Beau and Jane, who are in love and love her back? It would be more certain than a life with me. I'm always going to be the woman who faked her death and went into hiding and, yes, abandoned her daughter to do it.

Paige stirs and I wrap my arms around her and shift her closer. It hurts as much now as it did when I first left her. Picturing it again makes my throat ache with unshed tears.

I would do it. I would let her have her life here, if that would be better. I have to admit that it might be. Tearing her out of her life to be with me is what I want. It's not necessarily what's best for her.

When I was pregnant with Paige, other women used to say that having a child was like discovering a whole new kind of love. I never liked that description. I'd loved a lot in my life, and it seemed to cheapen that. They were right, in the end. It's not like any other love. I'd do anything for Paige. I'd break my own heart. I'd make myself miserable. I'd spend every day aching to see her and forcing myself not to, if that's what she needed.

I would do it even if it killed me.

"Not tonight," I whisper to the quiet. I'm not leaving her tonight. Tonight, I'm going to lie next to her in the bed and listen to her breathe. I'm so lucky. We were separated, but it wasn't permanent. Beau and Jane got her out of the fire. Her little heart is still beating, and still hopeful. It's all I hear as I fall asleep.

CHAPTER TWENTY-FOUR

Beau Rochester

ALL I WANT is to be with Jane.

There's movement behind her door when I arrive. It's cracked open, light spilling out into the hall. Jane steps in front of the door as I come in, a top in her hands. She's shaking it out, but she freezes when she sees me. Then she's back in motion again. I take it in. The suitcase. The clothes. A hurt red in her cheeks.

"What the hell is this?"

"I'm leaving," she announces.

"Like hell you are. Causey's done." I feel as light as I ever have. Joe was a piece of shit in school. He and my brother made life hell for everyone. It's done now. What's he going to do from a jail cell in the county building? Nothing.

Jane smooths the shirt into the suitcase. She shakes her head. "You don't need me anymore."

I thought I might find her already asleep. I thought I might find her staring at the ceiling, trying to process everything that happened. Or reading a book. I didn't think I'd find her in a hurry to get out of here. My chest aches, emotion threatening to overwhelm me. "Yes I do."

Jane doesn't answer. I'll be damned if she's not going to answer. I move behind her and turn her to face me. I can tell she's been crying. No tears now, just determination in her shining brown eyes.

"I need you," I insist. It comes out more intense than I meant it to. I don't know how to tell a woman I need her. I don't know how to tell her so she'll believe me. Adding anything else won't make a difference.

Her chest hitches. "I can't stand to watch you be with her."

"What the hell are you talking about?" Confusion stabs into my chest like a knife. The wounds it leaves are angry. She came back. She said she'd stay. All of it is unraveling in my hands, and for what?

"Paige has her mother back." Jane's lip quivers. "She doesn't need a nanny."

"Damn it, Jane, she doesn't need me either." I'm rougher than I want to be, but I can't stop myself. It's too damn late. Late in the day, and late in this thing we've done together. I'm not giving it up now. "She has her parent back, and I—" It descends on me all at once. The grief. It's heavy as a wave crashing into rock. It stops my heart. "I'm going to miss the hell out of her. I'm going to miss being—" I'm going to say being her dad, but I never was her dad, not really. "I'm going to miss being there for her. I'm going to miss it so damn much." The words don't stop coming. "I love her. I felt like her father. I didn't think it would end like this."

Jane's hands come up to my face. She's the sweetest woman on the planet. Here she is, in her own pain, and she's thinking about mine. Soothing mine away with a soft touch. "Maybe you are her dad," she offers.

"Actually." My throat tightens around a knot of truth. "I had a DNA test done. I'm not."

"Oh," Jane says, the sound full of compassion, and she pulls me down into her. "I know how much you wanted that," she whispers into my ear.

And damn it, I lose it.

I don't know whether it's tears or just pure salt and disappointment that run down my cheeks. Jane kisses me through them, her mouth soft and pliant on mine. It hurts so goddamn much. All of this has hurt since the very beginning. I never imagined that the best possible outcome would feel like drowning.

Jane's skin lets me breathe. We shed our clothes and go to the bed, which is soft and clean, like she is. I Inhale her skin and taste each of her nipples, and it keeps my lungs from collapsing. She keeps brushing at my cheeks with her fingertips. I find the soft curve of her stomach and lose myself in it. When Rhys died, when I got Paige, I didn't think the pain and the regret would ever end. They're still here. But I can see the other side.

"I'm going to miss her too," she says into the air. Jane keeps her voice low so she doesn't wake anybody up. There's one person she's bringing back to life. Me. I raise my head to look into her eyes. They're glistening with tears. "I had a dream—I thought the three of us could be a family together."

The admission tears my heart in two. I want to give this woman everything, but I can't give her this. We just have to be in this loss together. "It would have been good," I agree. "I wanted that too." I press a kiss below her belly button. "It doesn't make up for it, sweetheart, but I could give you something else."

Through her sadness, her eyes heat. "Make me feel good, Beau."

I put my hands on her hips. Slide them down to her thighs. "Tell me how you want it." Anything, Jane Mendoza. "My mouth? My cock?"

"Mouth first," she whispers.

She's soft and wet and ready for me, and if Jane Mendoza wants me to lick her until we both die of old age, then fine. Her hips work in a rhythm that's uniquely hers. My Jane is a searcher. She's always looking for more. I can give her more. My tongue in the folds of her. My tongue in her slit. She's sweet and salt and it's a salve over the wound in my chest from tonight's realization. Jane makes small noises and begs for more. This is what I want to drown in, not guilt. Not regret. Her. I ONLY WANT YOU. I write it again and again and again. I ONLY WANT YOU. ONLY YOU. ONLY YOU. ONLY YOU.

Jane makes a sound of longing, her hands reaching for my hair. My face. I make her come again before I let her pull me away from her. Anguish suffuses her touch now.

"I don't have to stop, sweetheart."

"I'm empty," she pants. I can't fix the loss of Paige we'll have to face. I can't replace it with anything else. But I can give her this. I can make this one aching thing feel better.

Between her thighs is the only place I can stand to be right now. She licks at my bottom lip while I fill her up. When I kiss her back, I don't know if the salt is from her tears or mine. The warmth of her body around me comforts a primal urge to back away from all this feeling. My love was dangerous for so long. To me. To everyone else. I never thought I'd feel this kind of obsessive love again, but it's here. With Jane, it takes on a new character. It is dangerous to love someone. Risky as all hell. Same as walking along a cliff's edge. Same as running. But there's only one place to fall now, and that's into her.

Jane clings to me like I'm a boat in a storm. It's the same for her, then. She's been looking for safe harbor. Maybe she thought she wanted total independence. The kind you can only get when you're by yourself. Her touch wants me. It seeks me, over and over, holding me to her. I'm not the one who was packing my suitcase, but I let her do it. I want her to reach for me. The sensation of her drowns the fear that says she shouldn't.

Our rhythm is broken up with sadness, but it works. It's a choppy, sorrowful thing we're doing. And hot, too. Her body's heat feels like so much more than mine. Enough to burn. Warm the ocean outside until it won't hurt to dive in. Jane sucks in a little breath and clenches around me.

"That's it," I murmur into her ear. "Come on my cock."

"You," she says. "You." No more words. Unnecessary.

I tease the side of her neck with my teeth and slip a hand between us. I-L-O-V-E-Y-O-U, I write on her clit. It makes her come in a shuddering moan that's made rich by her tears. Pleasure and pain are both pouring out of her now. One of her hands on my shoulder tells me what else she needs. My touch. My cock. Only me. I don't feel steady enough to deserve her, but Jane doesn't care. Her nails dig into my skin like I'm all that's left in the world.

She's all that's left in my world. The rest is coming apart. What puts me back together is her pleasure. She arches toward my touch, slick between our bodies, and when she comes it's with a low cry that sounds like both sadness and hope.

"Now you," she begs.

It feels almost like giving in, but I can't help it with Jane. I never have been able to. I love her so much. Damn her. She hooks her legs around my hips and holds me inside of her. I've never had pleasure torn from me in the middle of so much grief. It's an unburdening and acceptance all at once. Nobody ever makes it through these things unscathed. Missing Paige is going to hurt like hell. But we'll survive it. As long as I have Jane, I can survive anything.

We lie in the sheets for a long time. A thousand thoughts float across my mind. None of them seem worth breaking the silence for. I just listen to her breathe. For a while, it sounds like she might start crying again. It levels off. Smooths out. Jane rests her head against me and falls asleep.

CHAPTER TWENTY-FIVE

Jane Mendoza

SOMETIMES YOU COME to Maine on a cold, rainy day and end up taking care of a waterlogged kitten. Other times, you come downstairs with your former boss's hand on your lower back to find his brother's widow in the kitchen of the inn, making scrambled eggs while that same kitten looks on.

Paige sits at the kitchen island like a tiny queen. "It's good, Mom," she proclaims.

Emily gives us a sheepish wave. "I thought about pancakes, but I didn't want to go through all the cupboards. Eggs seemed easier."

She stayed here last night. Looking at her here with Paige, it was clearly the right choice. Paige eats her scrambled eggs with a rapturous expression, her blue eyes on Emily. We sit down with them and drink coffee.

All of us try to ignore the conversation we need to have.

When the dishes are in the dishwasher, and everything's clean, Emily pushes her hair back from her face. "Should we talk at the beach?"

"Good a place as any."

Paige is thrilled with the idea of the beach. She has plans for another sandcastle. The sunscreen and changing of clothes is less thrilling. There's some extra jostling and awkwardness while Emily and I try to negotiate who should do which thing. Paige wants me to do her sunscreen, but she wants Emily to help with her bathing suit. This is the last time I'll do her sunscreen, I think. And then I can't stop thinking it. This is the last time I'll find her bathing suit in the dryer. This is the last time I'll hand her a small plastic shovel that got lost under the couch.

It's breezy by the time the three of us follow her down to the beach. Paige stakes out the plot for her castle and fills her bucket with water. We pull in three beach chairs to her spot, Beau and I on one side, and Emily a little apart. Her eyes drink in every move Paige makes. I can't imagine how much she missed this. I can only imagine how much I'm going to.

When Paige is thoroughly absorbed in building her sandcastle, Beau clears his throat. "She should be with you, Emily."

Her eyes snap to his. "What?"

"Paige should go with you. She belongs with you. She's missed you, and she loves you, and you're alive."

Emily swallows hard. Her eyes go back to Paige, and it's a long, heavy minute before she speaks.

"I want her to be with me. Of course I do. I want that more than anything. But I think—" My heart hurts for her. Every word she says sounds harder to say than the last. "I think there's an argument to be made that she'd be better off with you and Jane. If that's what you think, then I would agree to that. For her."

Somehow, her eyes have landed on me. I'm the one with the least power in this situation. I don't have custody of Paige in any way. But it almost feels like Emily is asking my permission. It feels heavy, to have her asking me this. Like I'm weighing the entire world. Beau could keep her, if he wanted to. He could make Emily fight him for custody and hold on to Paige until the bitter end. Bitter doesn't begin to describe how it would be. It would be worse than bitter. And even if Emily did agree to have Paige stay, I know it would break her heart. I know it. She would never be the same.

"No," I say, and Emily exhales. "She's yours."

"I'm so grateful," she says breathlessly. "I'm so grateful to the two of you for taking care of her. And for giving her back to me."

"It's the right thing." Beau's tone is final, but it's rough. This conversation is so hard. We all want what's best for Paige. It doesn't make this process less painful.

"I'm not leaving," Emily mentions suddenly. "I hope you know."

"You're not leaving the inn?"

"I'm not leaving Eben Cape. I'll obviously find another place to live—somewhere that's good for Paige—but I'm not going to take her away from everything she knows. That includes you. Both of you."

Beau reaches for my hand and squeezes it tight. "Emily."

"I mean it." Emily wipes at her eyes. "I don't know what that looks like. I don't even know if you're planning to stay here. We'll figure it out. I'm not taking a damn thing away from her."

Emily looks so small and alone, sitting by herself. I can't look at her for another second, so I let go of Beau's hand and go over to her. It's only human to give her a hug.

She laughs, her voice quivery, but her arms go around me too. "She loves you, Jane."

"She's missed you so much."

"Why are you hugging?" Paige stands a couple of feet off, her arms crossed over her chest. A red sand shovel pokes up from one fist. "You both look sad."

"We're not sad," I say. It's half-true. I'm so glad for Paige that she has her mother back. And I'm so sad that the dream I had—of a family with her and Beau—won't look the same as I pictured.

Paige looks between Emily and me, and then she runs forward and wedges herself between us. It's the kind of hug that only a seven-year-old can give, slightly gangly and too tight. Oh—this is how it will work, then. Paige will be so happy, and that's what will matter beyond everything else. The hard conversations and awkward moments will fade into the background.

I take a breath that feels lighter for the first time in days. I didn't know how much I wanted to watch her grow up until I thought Beau and I were giving her up forever. The thought of never seeing her again tore my heart in two. But getting to see her be with her mom and find happiness again? It will be better than anything I could have imagined.

"Come see my sandcastle," Paige orders. "It has four towers and four walls. I'm thinking of adding another courtyard."

Then she runs back to her work, trusting us to follow her. And we do. There was a brief moment in time where this girl was an orphan. She was alone, like me. But there's a happier ending for her. She has her mother back. And more than that, she has Beau and me. We'll always be here for her, whatever she needs. She has more family than she knows what to do with. It's a fairy tale ending for an orphan. My father didn't come back from the dead, but I still got my happy ending. I have Paige and even Emily. I have Beau, who's become more than my lover. He's my family. My everything. My safe harbor in the storm.

CHAPTER TWENTY-SIX

Jane Mendoza

THE FIRST THING I do when everything is apply to colleges.

I apply to several in Maine. And even one back in Texas, one that had been on my list of dream colleges. It feels surreal when the acceptance letters start coming in.

Beau promises that we can go anywhere, but I know he's worried about being so far away from Paige. I'm worried about it, too. Not for Paige's sake. She has her mother back. It's more about me and Beau. We love Paige. The exact parameters of that love are hazy. Does Beau love her like a father or like an uncle? Do I love her like a mother or a nanny? Precision doesn't matter when it comes to love. The fact is, we want to be able to see her.

So I accept an offer to join an online program at a small university in Maine. That way we can live in Eben Cape while I get my degree. I can still drive for an hour when I need to meet with my advisor or attend a lecture in person.

Beau turns his attention to building us a house.

It's only half a mile down the coast from Coach House.

The trees drop their leaves not long after the fall semester starts, and in the winter the unfinished frame looks like a gingerbread house. He installs gorgeous hardwood and solid doors like we had at Coach House. It's smaller, though. Cozier. Warmer.

It's more than a house. It's a home. A family.

Because Beau is there.

"Tell me everything," he always says, the moment I emerge from my study. And then he listens, his dark eyes on my face, intent as I tell him about some study I read about or some test I'm making. Only when I'm finished does he pull me close and kiss me.

We get to see Paige all the time, almost every day. She's in school again and making new friends. I know it's good for her to be with her mother most of the time, and to be back in regular school, but I miss having her around all the time. It's quiet in the house.

Sometimes I feel guilty for having so much.

I always knew that if I went to college, it would be hard. Really hard. There's a reason why such a tiny percentage of people who age out of the foster care system finish college. We don't have a support system. We don't have money. We don't have anything.

Survival is the only thing we can manage.

If I hadn't met Beau, I'd have to work multiple jobs to pay for classes and stay up late studying. I was willing to do it, though. I was willing to be bone-tired and worn thin by the end if it meant I'd get my degree. It meant that much to me.

I do stay up late studying for classes. Not because I'm working two jobs, though.

Beau forbids me from getting a job at one of the cafés in town. I curl up on the couch with my books from class because I want to. At least once a week it makes my throat tight to think of how lucky I am. The girl I used to be would have done anything to have this life. I'd like to believe she would have gotten here eventually.

I hope she would have.

"It feels wrong," I admit to Beau halfway through my second year. "Like I'm not struggling enough for this. Like I should be doing more, or trying harder."

He leans against the countertop in our kitchen. Snow comes down outside in fat flakes. We're four days from winter break and all I want is to sleep in. My days are wall-to-wall busy with classes and study groups and reading textbooks.

"You made the dean's list again," he says. "What more do you think you need to do?"

He hung Christmas lights last week. They're multicolored, stretched across the roof of the porch. We live in this house on the coast with Christmas lights on the porch. "Maybe I don't deserve it. It was going to be a difficult thing, you know?"

He wraps an arm around my waist and pulls me in for a kiss. "You don't have to suffer for something to be worth it. You deserve peace."

Hearing him say it goes straight to my heart. "I thought it would be kind of awful and exhausting, but then I'd have earned it."

"You did earn it."

"But—"

"You earned it with every book you read, every test you take. You earn it with every ounce of determination in your beautiful little body. Now, do you want to argue or do you want to go to bed?"

"It's too early to go to bed."

"It's too early to go to *sleep*. I have other plans for you."

How am I supposed to resist him when he's like this?

The first year finishes. I'm not much older than my classmates, but I'm the only one who lives so far away from campus. Most of the students in my study group live in the city. They rent apartments together. They attend parties. I expect to feel jealous that I'm missing out on that part of the college experience, but I don't. I like Beau's steadiness. He's there for me whenever I need him. No frat party with red cups could compare with that.

In the second year, we have to choose an internship. I land one at a local charity that puts together welcome baskets for foster children. So often they show up at temporary homes with no extra clothes, no toothbrushes, nothing. The baskets include the necessities, along with a teddy bear. It's the hardest work I've ever done, and I'm only an intern.

What I find is that every case is as emotionally charged as it was with Paige when I first came to Coach House. Tensions run high in the families we work with. In the children who have to be placed into foster care, but also in the parents. Everyone struggles. My days are filled with shadowing placement calls and picking up supplies and going over paperwork that my boss delegates to me. There is a lot of paperwork, and it's always changing.

Kids have to be moved from one place to another. They always need things.

It's heartbreaking to see them. Their worry. Their anger. Their fear.

I arrive home one spring evening with red, swollen eyes. Swiping at them with the back of my hand does nothing. Beau's going to know I was crying. I don't want him to think this is too much for me. I don't want him to think I'm not happy. But today was a tough one.

It was a boy who'd come into the system right when I was starting my internship. I'd given him the basket, then returned the next day with a deck of cards. He wanted to be a magician, he said, so that he could be invisible. He guessed which card I picked out of the deck.

He must have ended up back with his birth parents. That's the ending we hope for with foster care, if the parents are alive. That they'll be returned. But so often it doesn't work. The parents relapse. The neglect continues. Or worse.

That night he shows up again, his cheek darkened with a bruise.

Beau's lamp is on in his office as I climb the steps, but he meets me at the door. Wordlessly, he takes me into his arms and holds me tight.

"You know," I say, my voice thick. "This was my dream."

I didn't know it would feel like this to achieve everything I ever wanted. I didn't know it would involve red eyes and an aching heart. I didn't realize, somehow, that it would mean missing all these kids I've worked with. This is only an internship. If I keep doing this, it'll mean years of saying goodbye. Years of sad memories.

"Is it still your dream?"

"Yes. But I thought I'd be able to turn it off somehow."

"You, turn off your heart? That's what makes you so good at this. The day you stop feeling things is the day you should retire."

"I never want to retire. The work is too important."

"One day you might."

"Not any day soon."

"They're new beginnings," he says. "All those goodbyes. They're a fresh start for those kids. Every time you let one of them go, it's to start a new life."

I have a new life now. "Thank you."

"You'll make it," he says, as if he's reading my mind. "I've got you."

"What about you?" I pull back to look into his face. At the dark eyes that stole my heart at Coach House and won't ever give it back again. "Are you happy like this?"

"Yes," he says without reservation.

He still does some work on his investments, but most of his time has gone towards working with the builders to get it done quickly. With furnishing the new house. With taking care of Paige when she comes over after school. With taking care of me between online classes.

His phone starts ringing in his pocket, and he groans. "I wanted to be inside you."

"I just got home."

"Exactly." He takes one look at the screen and declines the call. "Work can wait. You. Naked. On the bed. I'm going to kiss your sweet cunt until you forget everything but my name."

And he does.

EPILOGUE

Jane Mendoza

THE NEW HOUSE is where everything happens.

It's where I take classes from a sunny office Beau built for me and do my homework at the kitchen table when I want a change of scenery. It's the first new house I've ever lived in, and even after months of waking up here and going to sleep, it still smells new. And fresh. Everything is possible here.

We live in sight of Coach House, where Paige lives with Emily. We've all got breathing room, but not real distance. I'm not done with my degree yet, but it's a living example of all the shapes a family can take. Sometimes we focus too hard on two parents and two-point-five kids.

The family that I have fulfills every hole inside my heart.

I'm at the kitchen table reading case notes for

my schoolwork. I've only got about a minute to go, and so much to read. So much to know. I'm excited to start a career but I don't ever want to stop learning. These kids deserve that much from me.

Paige bursts through the door, bringing the breeze with her. Her backpack knocks against her back, and Kitten, who is no longer a kitten, follows her inside. "Jane! I've been waiting all day to tell you about chess club."

"I can't wait to hear it." I poke my head out the door and wave in the direction of Coach House, the sign I'm taking over. Emily will be watching to make sure Paige makes it safely. Then I shut the door and turn to Paige for a hug. "Important question. Popcorn first or Monopoly first?"

"Both, obviously." Paige does an eye-roll that makes me laugh. She's moved onto chess as her primary focus, but she still loves Monopoly. "And I want to stay up late."

"Staying up late is a guarantee." For two reasons. I'll stay up talking to Paige as long as she wants. There's another reason I don't get much sleep lately...

A small cry from the stairs.

Beau's coming down with the baby on his

arm. Baby fists stretch in the air. He's still rubbing his eyes, mewling and confused from his nap.

"I did warn you about the binky situation," Beau says to the baby, his voice as measured as if he was speaking to a grown up. No baby talk from this man. "I warned you that it would lead to a shorter nap, and it did. That's okay though. We learn more when we experiment. Are you a scientist? I think you are." Beau looks up from the baby and his eyes light up. "And Paige is here. Tell me you chose a good movie."

Paige runs to his side and squeezes him around the waist. "I picked the best movie. It has robots and emojis and a princess who has a sword. But you don't care what it is."

"I just care that we're here," Beau says. "That we're together."

She gives him a big grin before cooing over the baby. "Hello, little Bastian. Are you sleepy? Did you miss me? We're going to hang out *all night.* No sleeping."

"Don't encourage him," Beau says, his voice dry.

Paige curls up beside Bastian's ocean-themed gym, and Beau sets the baby down. He kicks, a little disoriented, until Paige makes the octopus twirl in the air. She's not quite old enough to walk around with the baby, but she can hold him when they're both on the ground. They're thick as thieves, those two. I already know that Paige will spend most of her time here cooing over the baby. It makes my heart clench to see them, every time. I grew up in house full of children, but we weren't siblings. We didn't feel like brothers and sisters. We felt like prisoners, trapped and lashing out. Seeing Paige and Bastian spend time together fills the empty spaces in my past. Family isn't about blood. It's about love.

Beau joins me in the kitchen. "Did you finish?"

I'm working on reading assignments and essays. Those things I understand. It's hard, but I can pour myself into school. I can get As, which makes me feel good. Beau takes me out to a fancy dinner in Dover every time I finish midterms.

The past few weeks have been different.

I was asked to give a talk to a group of girls in a group home. I wanted to say no. It felt like too much responsibility. Then I looked into Beau's steady, storm-gray eyes, and I knew that it was exactly the right amount of responsibility. It would be hard, but I could do. I *must* do it, because those kids deserve my best.

Even if it means working through the night for a week.

Wordlessly, I hand over a sheet of paper.

I've written the speech a hundred times. Each time I scratch things out and rewrite. The wastebasket is filled with crumpled notebook paper.

Beau reads. His dark eyebrows go up. "Jane."

"Is it bad?"

"Jane."

"It's the worst thing you've ever read."

He looks at the paper again. "*Only three percent of kids who age out of the foster care system ever get a college degree. I was going to be in that three percent even if it killed me… And it almost did kill me. That put things into perspective. College is important, but I learned that living's important, too. Your life has value whether or not you have that piece of paper. I don't want you to be part of the three percent. I want you to be part of the six percent. The twenty percent. I want you to change the number, but more than that, I want you to know that you matter. Your life matters. It can be hard to remember that when our mom or dad isn't around to tell us. That's why I'm here today. To tell you that I'm proud of you. You're not a college diploma or a first-place medal from a track meet or a perfect attendance record. You're not the sum total of your achievements. You're a living, breathing person, and your value is simply... you. So strive and work and study, but know that already, already you're enough."*

My cheeks are flushed pink by the time he finishes. "Beau."

"You're enough," he murmurs, as if I might not know. Because I don't. I told those kids what I needed to hear when I was their age. It's still what I need to hear. "You're perfect."

He drags me into his arms, squeezing so tight I run out of air. It's perfect. Exactly what I need. Always. Forever. "Love you," I breathe out.

His hand slips beneath my soft, slouchy T-shirt. He speaks to me in the most private way, through the words he writes on my skin. L O V E Y O U T O O.

THE END

Thank you so much for reading the Rochester trilogy! If you love Beau and Jane, I have great news for you. You can get a bonus scene if you sign up for my newsletter...

GO HERE: www.skyewarren.com/rochester

I've been wanting to write a Jane Eyre retelling forever. So when Radish asked me if I could write more about these characters, I thought it was the perfect way to show what happens "after the end" as well as what happens to Emily and Mateo.

And of course Paige!

It's completely optional for you to keep reading. I want all my readers to feel comfortable stopping at book three if they want to do that.

I love the exclusive material I'm writing for Radish, but it's not required.

What is Radish? It's a serialized reading app where you can read books an episode at a time. If you want to read more, find Radish Fiction by searching on the App Store and Google Play.

Once you download, simply type 'Hiding Places' into the Radish search bar. Radish Fiction is your destination for Romance!

To get free coupons to read Hiding Places, go to www.skyewarren.com/radish and open the Radish download link and sign up to receive free episodes.

I'm also writing the story of Marjorie, who owns the Lighthouse Inn…

Marjorie Dunn is hiding in plain sight. The past can't find her at the peaceful inn she owns in a quiet coastal town in Maine.

Until Sam Brewer walks through the door. He arrives in the dead of night, with a dark suit and storm-gray eyes.

Marjorie knows better than to trust this stranger, but she can't resist his touch. Every kiss binds them together. Every night draws the danger close.

She risks her heart with him, but more than that, she risks her life.

The past has caught up with her. And it wants her dead.

Books by Skye Warren

Endgame Trilogy & more books in Tanglewood
The Pawn
The Knight
The Castle
The King
The Queen
Escort
Survival of the Richest
The Evolution of Man
Mating Theory
The Bishop

North Security Trilogy & more North brothers
Overture
Concerto
Sonata
Audition
Diamond in the Rough
Silver Lining
Gold Mine

Finale

Chicago Underground series
Rough
Hard
Fierce
Wild
Dirty
Secret
Sweet
Deep

Stripped series
Tough Love
Love the Way You Lie
Better When It Hurts
Even Better
Pretty When You Cry
Caught for Christmas
Hold You Against Me
To the Ends of the Earth

For a complete listing of Skye Warren books, visit
www.skyewarren.com/books

About the Author

Skye Warren is the New York Times bestselling author of dangerous romance. Her books have sold over one million copies. She makes her home in Texas with her loving family, sweet dogs, and evil cat.

Sign up for Skye's newsletter:
www.skyewarren.com/newsletter

Like Skye Warren on Facebook:
facebook.com/skyewarren

Join Skye Warren's Dark Room reader group:
skyewarren.com/darkroom

Follow Skye Warren on Instagram:
instagram.com/skyewarrenbooks

Visit Skye's website for her current booklist:
www.skyewarren.com

Copyright

This is a work of fiction. Any resemblance to actual persons, living or dead, business establishments, events or locales is entirely coincidental. All rights reserved. Except for use in a review, the reproduction or use of this work in any part is forbidden without the express written permission of the author.

Best Kept Secret © 2021 by Skye Warren
Print Edition

Cover design by Book Beautiful